FORBIDDEN MUSIC

It was the most beautiful music Flutirr had ever heard. Somewhere in the deep shadowy corners of his mind, he knew that no other High Noble would ever accept such a piece. Just a few weeks ago, he himself would have been disgusted by it. But he had changed. He no longer cared so much about petty mathematical definitions of music.

At first he merely sat, swaying in time to the music. Then he had the insight that the music was a celebration of the sun. He could not explain how he had reached that feeling; it had come unbidden to him. This piece far surpassed any of the Noblish songs he had played in school on either harp or flute. It caused an ache in him, a tingling in his fingers, and he sorely wished he could play along with this Nelvin.

The song faded away, and Flutirr opened his eyes. The Nelvin was crossing the bridge. Flutirr froze—he must not see him, he must not see him, he mustn't . . .

It was too late . . .

And Don't Miss These Other
AVON FLARE COMPETITION *Winners*

AT THE EDGE
by Michael Behrens

BUCK
by Tamela Larimer

DRAGON FALL
by Lee J. Hindle

WINNER
OF THE
AVON FLARE
COMPETITION

Flute Song
Magic

ANDREA SHETTLE

AN AVON FLARE BOOK

FLUTE SONG MAGIC is an original publication of Avon Books. This work has never before appeared in book form.

AVON BOOKS
A division of
The Hearst Corporation
105 Madison Avenue
New York, New York 10016

To George and Constance Farnham, for raising my mother, and for cheering me on through the years.

To my parents, for learning sign language when I was three years old, and still without language. For spending day after day teaching me two words—"ap[ple]" and "up"—so I could go on to learn all the thousands of words I needed to know to write this book.

To all the sign language interpreters who enabled me to be mainstreamed with my hearing peers in public schools, in order to receive a challenging education—and also to all the fellow students who helped me out by taking notes for me in class.

To my sister, Cindy, who often acted as my "buffer" and interpreter while I was growing up in a hearing world.

To Anne Serafin, for helping me improve my writing skills during junior year English, and making thousands of helpful comments—big and small—on *Flute Song Magic*.

To Gallaudet University, the only liberal arts college for the deaf in the world, for providing an environment where those of us who are deaf can participate fully in life, while learning about our complex language of American Sign Language and the richness and diversity of our cultural community.

Just so I can see her face when she reads this: Hi, Ann Long!

Prologue

FLUTIRR wanted his mommy. He was tired and confused, and only his mother's safe, warm lap could make him feel better. He started tramping through the house, looking for her. He would find her, then he would tell her about everything that had happened that day. He would tell her about what he had seen and the frightening things Daddy had told him afterward. Then Mommy would let him crawl into her lap and hold him until his scared feeling went away and the dark, hollow pair of eyes he had looked into that day stopped haunting him.

He and Daddy had been downtown when it happened.

First, Flutirr had detected a warm, breadlike, nutty smell in the air.

Wild nut pastries! Flutirr had searched anxiously for the pastry stand he knew had to be there, but he couldn't find it. Too many people were in the street, and he was only a little boy unable to see over anyone's head.

Flutirr did what any little boy would do in such a dilemma: he grabbed his daddy's hand and gave it one good, firm yank. Then he looked straight up into Daddy's eyes with the most mournful look he could muster. He knew Daddy would fall for it. He was a *child*, after all. Children were given everything.

Daddy didn't smile—Daddy was a High Noble, and High Nobles never smiled. Even so, Flutirr thought he saw Daddy's eyes crinkle up just a little at the corners, so he knew he would get what he wanted. And sure enough, Daddy went right up to the pastry stand to buy him a wild nut pastry. The merchant, thank the Nobleness, was a Noble too, or Daddy couldn't have bought the pastry. Nobles couldn't buy from anyone from what Mommy and Daddy called the Lower Classes—it was dirty, and it could get you demoted to a lower class too, so you wouldn't be a Noble anymore.

They kept walking down the street while Flutirr ate his pastry. Then Flutirr saw the Nelvin.

The Nelvin was not an ordinary-looking Nelvin, like Flutirr and his daddy and all the other Nelvins in the street. He was a filthy, scrawny creature dressed in what must have been as many as a hundred pieces of cloth that magically clung to each other. The most perplexing thing about the Nelvin was that the pieces of cloth were all different colors. Flutirr knew that there were exactly nine classes of Nelvins, and each of them wore two colors as a symbol of rank. High Nobles like Flutirr and his daddy, for instance, got to wear purple and blue. So what class could this Nelvin possibly belong to?

The strange Nelvin put a harmonica to his mouth, and began to play. Flutirr, of course, had seen Nelvins make music before. He himself had tried dozens of instruments, just like every other Nelvin child. This Nelvin was already such a strange sight, however, that everything he did only emphasized his bizarreness. Flutirr was spellbound. And he was further enraptured when he heard the music itself: it was pretty, sparkling music. He had never heard the Nobles he knew play music like that—the sound was almost like water, the way it gurgled through the air.

A passing Nelvin did something very strange. She paused to reach into the bag she carried, then she threw a round slab of bread to the ground before hurrying down the street. The harmonica player abruptly stopped playing and pounced at the food. He tore a hefty piece from the loaf and chewed vigorously upon it, before pawing with his trembling hands at his own bag so he could open it and store the rest of his new treasure. Then the musician looked awkwardly at the Nelvins about him, as though he was ashamed and wished no one could see him. In that moment, he happened to see Flutirr watching him. The two Nelvins stared at each other, then the older Nelvin's eyes flooded with a blazing hatred.

Flutirr drew back, frightened. Why would this stranger hate him? What had he done? But wait—the hatred was fading away to be replaced with a silent apology, then with anguish. It frightened him as much as the anger had; he could not understand how anyone could feel so much pain.

He ran to his father's side and yanked his hand. "Who is that man, Daddy?"

Flutirr's father looked, and suddenly stiffened. For an instant, Flutirr thought he actually saw his father frown. His daddy *never* frowned. High Nobles like him and Daddy were not supposed to frown. Then the frown vanished, and his father said harshly: "There is no one there."

That, of course, made no sensè, for there was the Nelvin right there, playing his harmonica again. "He's right *there*, Daddy—he's playing the harmonica. Who is he?" Flutirr was prepared to spend the rest of the afternoon badgering away until he got his answer. His father must have known it, for he abruptly pulled Flutirr away and stormed down the street with him until they came upon a quiet area with no other Nelvin in sight. Father and son alike paused to catch their breaths, then the father gave Flutirr a stern look. "Flutirr. I am about to tell you something that you must never forget, because I can never say it to you again. Do you understand?"

"Yes, Dad—Noble—Noble Father."

"That—Nelvin—does not exist. As a Noble, you must never speak of him, or of those like him."

"But—who—wh—"

Flutirr's father crouched on his haunches so he could look directly into Flutirr's eyes. "Flutirr—do you remember what your mother and I told you about all the races of Trillilani?"

Flutirr racked his memory. There were Nelvins—the most superior race of all—and the Elvins, Kuu, Dwalines, and Humans. And those were just the races Nelvins knew about. Trillilani was so large you could ride a horse for ten years in any direction and still not come to the end of it—so how could anyone know what else was out there? Trillilani was so big it was infi—infin—

"Infinite. That's good, Flutie," his father had said. Then he had gone on to explain about the classless ones—about the Nelvin-like creatures like the beggar they had just seen. "They are so different from Nelvins they are like another race, Flutie. They are even worse than any of the eight classes below High Nobles, because, as you know, Respectables and Tolerables, at least, can try to be just as good as Nobles. If they succeed, they can be promoted to a higher class. These classless vermin can never do that. Once you are demoted so low you have no class anymore, there is no hope. You can never be as good as a Noble, or even a Respectable or a Tolerable—and neither can your children, your grandchildren, or the great-great-grandchildren of your great-great-grandchildren. Do you understand, Flutie?" Flutirr understood.

"That is why you must never speak of the classless ones, Flutie. Just to speak of them is even worse than speaking directly to a Tolerable. Only speak of them when you must tell your own children of these creatures—then never again."

Flutirr gestured to show that he understood. He knew that speaking to a Tolerable could get you demoted so low you became a Tolerable yourself. If even referring to the classless ones was as terrible a crime as his father made it sound, then the punishment was probably demotion to classless status. Flutirr shuddered. He did not ever want to be classless like that poor, starved-looking Nelvin who had looked at him with those dark eyes.

So Flutirr had been frightened that day, and needed his mommy's lap. He kept searching for his mother and found her, finally, in the workroom. She was busily drawing lines and symbols in the mysterious process grown-ups called writing. He promptly went to her and started crawling into her lap, head first.

To his profound puzzlement, he found himself rudely shoved away. "Don't do that, Flutirr," he was told. Flutirr wavered on his feet a moment, then tried again. He simply could not believe that the event of the previous moment had ever occurred. It was like looking up at the sky and seeing four moons instead of the three you knew existed. If you thought you saw something that clearly couldn't be there, then the only thing to do was to disregard the erroneous data.

The erroneous data, however, chose to repeat itself. Once again, he was shoved away from the soft lap that had always welcomed him so warmly in the past. "Don't, Flutirr," said the cold voice that knew how to be warm and soothing.

"Mommy—"

"You are a High Noble, Flutirr. You are one of the most superior members of the Nelvin race. And you are also almost six years old, Flutirr, and will be starting school soon. It is time you learned to behave like a proper Noble—and proper, grown-up Nobles do not crawl into their mothers' lap for comfort.''

"Mama—" In his voice was despair. He did not understand it. Tilirrri from just a few mansions down the street was a High Noble too, and he was almost *nine*—yet his parents still touched him, and sometimes even smiled at him. So he asked his mama about Tilirrri.

His mother's chin only became harder at Flutirr's pleading tone. "If Tilirrri's parents choose to treat him like that, that is their choice. In this family, your father and I think it is time you began to practice High Noble behavior. Anyone who has learned what your father tells me you learned today is ready to begin. Proper Nobles, for instance, address their parents as either 'Mother and Father' or 'Noble Mother and Noble Father'—never as 'Mama and Daddy.' " Then Flutirr's mother's voice became sharp: "Must you always be so much more emotional than other Noble children? You know Nobles never cry."

Flutirr tried his best to contain the tears that were steaming down his face. "Y-yes, Noble Mother," he said. What he meant was: Yes, I will learn Noble behavior. I will never try to touch you, or anyone else, again. I will also never cry again, even if my own life is in danger.

But he still, so sorely, ached for his mother's lap. And just a few weeks later, he failed.

It happened at school. It was the first day of school for all the children, so of course none of them was

7

very Noblish that day. For twenty chaotic minutes, they all ran helter-skelter about the field where their classes were to be held, shouting and playing with one another. The Instructors let them; even they remembered what it was like to be a child. All of the children took the chance to be boisterous—except, of course, for Flutirr.

The night before, Flutirr's parents had carefully coached him on the proper Noblish behavior for a Noble child going to school. Ignore the other children when they act silly and unNoblish, they had told him. In time, their parents will teach them to be Noblish too—but *you* are starting to learn now. *You* must walk quietly and solemnly to school like a good Noblish boy. When you arrive, you must go to the Head Instructor of all the High Noble children, and say to her, "I am Flutirr-Sinie-Tilll, and I am pleased to be at school learning the things I will need to know to be a Noblish High Noble." Then you must give her this note, so she will know you are not to be treated like other six-year-old High Noble children—the teachers are to expect more of you. You are to be fully Noblish.

So he sat on the ground, as he had been told, and he acted Noblish. He did not laugh, and he certainly did not cry. Just like a really big High Noble boy, he thought to himself proudly. Not like the little children who played all around him.

Still, he was glad when some of the other children stopped to speak to him. It made him feel less lonely, even if they only stopped to say: "C'mon let's play together." Because, of course, he had to respond, "I cannot play today. Playing is too unNoblish."

That caused a minor commotion.

"Even my big sister doesn't have to be Noblish yet, and she's eight."

"My brother's bigger than that—he's ten. Mommy and Daddy say he started being just a little Noblish at seven all by himself, and now he's all the way Noblish."

"Well, *my* daddy knows Flutirr's mommy and daddy, and *he* says Flutirr must be really bad, or really unNoblish, if his mom and dad want him to be Noblish already."

"I am *not* unNoblish," Flutirr said. This was going all wrong. His friends were supposed to envy him, to be jealous of him, for being grown-up enough to act Noblish.

"Yes, you are—look, you're crying, that's unNoblish. Even I don't cry anymore." The other children promptly agreed; Flutirr was scrunching up his face so much he *had* to be crying.

"I am *not* crying," Flutirr said, and immediately burst into tears. Unfortunately for Flutirr, the Head Instructor had been watching. She promptly swooped down upon the frightened Flutirr and dragged him to the front of the class. Flutirr stood, checking himself over for invisible bruises, while she made everyone sit on the ground so they could start listening. She was going to talk about marks today, she said.

"Now, most of your parents have already told you about marks. If they did, they probably told you that you mostly have to worry about the yellow marks you get every day in class for small mistakes. Most of you will get gray marks only by first getting many, many yellow marks—it is very bad to get a gray mark in just one day at school. I am telling you this so you will understand why I am extremely disappointed that I must give a gray mark to a child in this class on his very first day at school.

"Flutirr, you are a big boy, and you are a High Noble—yet just a moment ago, I saw you crying like a Tolerable child. For that, I must give you one whole gray mark. Step closer, Flutirr."

Flutirr was mortified. Less than a day in school, and he was already a year behind—it was almost enough to make him start crying again. Instead, he obeyed; he stepped forward.

The Instructor spat. Twice. The moisture of her saliva thoroughly splattered Flutirr's face, so he bewilderedly tried to wipe it off. A gray mark must be even worse than he had thought—no one was supposed to spit on you unless you were from a lower class.

His classmates knew that as well as Flutirr did. They laughed at the bizarre sight of a High Noble child removing spit from his face. Horrified, Flutirr desperately started looking for his friends, for the children he had played with so often before. Surely one of them would look at him with sympathy and make him feel better.

But no. Wayni and Tillune were laughing with the

rest. Fruenillli wasn't laughing, but she wasn't looking at him either. No one was being his friend.

And then Flutirr instinctively knew: it was always going to be like this. They weren't going to forget—they would remember, and no one would be his friend fo a long time. No one would play with him, the suddenly Noblish boy with the gray mark. No one would talk to him, or walk with him on the way home from school. Then Flutirr thought of the classless one he had seen the other week, and for that moment, he understood him. He understood the pain he had seen in the dark eyes of the beggar, and the shame.

I am like you, he thought to the classless one. *I am feeling the way you feel.*

The black, anguished eyes of the classless one momentarily loomed in front of him before Flutirr blocked the image. It was an unNoblish thing to think of such a sight—and now Flutirr had a duty to prove all his friends wrong. He had to be forever Noblish.

Chapter 1

FLUTIRR strode down the street in the strong light of early afternoon right next to the market tables. He lifted his chin high and looked straight ahead, ignoring the impudent sales pitches of the merchants—one of them was as low as Tolerable class, in Nobleness's name! He was tempted to stop and scold the merchant's rudeness in addressing a High Noble, but he held himself back. As a High Noble, he simply couldn't violate the decree against direct communication between Nobles and Tolerables. The proper thing would be to report the Tolerable, but he couldn't do that without revealing his visit to this heterogeneous district. Such a visit wasn't illegal, but his parents certainly wouldn't approve of his being there without some good reason. It was infuriating, but he had to let the Tolerable get away with addressing him. He may well have been addressing someone else anyway—Flutirr was not the only one walking down the street.

The corners of his mouth nearly twitched upward—

but careful, he reminded himself, control the face, don't let the lower-class citizens see a Noble smile, especially not over something as insignificant as a pastry stand. Already he could smell his favorite childhood food—wild nut pastry, made with moist dough and crushed nuts imported from some distant Nelvin territory. But then he saw the vendor and his nascent smile faded. She was only a Mid Respectable. He could not legally speak with her or buy from her. He caught himself looking too long and hungrily at the food and forced himself to look away, head up, eyes ahead, to fool other Nelvins into thinking he had no interest in that table; after all, it was manned by a lower-class citizen.

Flutirr paused at the street corner to make sure no horses were coming, though it didn't seem as though even the Nobles or Respectables owned horses in this area. He tried, but failed, to ignore the Mid Tolerable beside him setting up his accordion. He turned and pretended to look at the brightly colored pieces of cloth laid out on the table at the corner. He was absently fingering a piece of blue cloth when the music began. He tried to maintain his pretense of ignoring the Tolerable, but within a single measure, his hands on the cloth were still with awe. By the second measure, his fingers were softly tapping in rhythm to the tune. Then Flutirr found his hands flitting to the harp he carried on his shoulder, wanting desperately to play along. But no, he could not and should not play such a sacrilegious piece in public. It did have rhythm, but it was not the Perfect rhythm taught to the Nobles in his school, and it was too infused with sentimental feelings to be proper for a Noble to play. He should not even be listening to this barbarous piece, and his parents would be furious to know he was even standing here at the table of a Low Respectable, listening to the lowly music of a Mid Tolerable.

Yet his fingers struggled to follow the song, silently touching the right stings yet hesitating to pluck them. He had been to this district a few times before, drawn by the unNoblish temptation of the lower-class music he knew he would find there—but this was the first time the music had been powerful enough to make his fingers want to follow along with the beat. It was then that he realized that the Mid Tolerable was playing in a strange rhythm unfamiliar to him. It was not 4/4 time, nor was it 2/4 time. So what could it be? Those were the only meters taught in his school; any other meter was denounced as being less than Perfect and not worth learning. Flutirr stood for a moment trying to puzzle it out, but couldn't. There seemed to be as many as six beats to each measure, yet it was played too quickly for 6/4 time. Obviously the only way he could get an answer to his questions was to ask the Mid Tolerable, but it was illegal for Flutirr to speak directly with him.

There was no way around it; he would have to set up a Class-to-Class Chain. It might mean talking with a High Respectable if he couldn't find a Low Noble, but that was only distasteful, not illegal. A few minutes' walk down a nearby side street revealed only a handful of High Respectables, all too young to leave their own yards let alone work a Chain. Further searching, however, turned up a young adolescent Low Noble showing off his sword to a cluster of High Respectables like someone who has just received a new toy.

"You there," Flutirr called, and all four boys glanced up. "Yes, you with the sword. I have an errand for you," he said.

"What kind of errand?" the Low Noble said, his tone unNoblishly offhand.

"Do your parents know you speak like that to sons of Vice Presidents on the High Council?" Flutirr said mildly, raising his eyebrows slightly.

"Well, what of it?" he shot back, but in a subdued manner more proper of a Noble—particularly one addressing a superior Noble. He even sheathed his sword. Flutirr resisted an urge to smirk. "What do you have for me . . . your Nobleness?"

"I am setting up a Chain to speak with a Mid Tolerable, and I will pay you seven Jublas for helping me."

"Eight. I'll do it for eight Jublas, your Nobleness."

Flutirr's chin lifted angrily, and a few nearly invisible muscles twitched, but otherwise he remained outwardly calm.

"Seven is a good price. No higher."

The Low Noble considered. "Well, I might accept seven and seven-eighth Jublas if I only need to speak to a Mid Respectable, rather than a Low Respectable," he said. An impudent grin tugged at the corners of his mouth, but did not quite escape. The boy was behaving, Flutirr thought irritably, very much like a Respectable who had recently been promoted and had yet to learn proper Noblish conduct. He had, at least, learned to indicate proper displeasure at the thought of speaking to a Nelvin too low in class—though, of course, he had conveniently neglected to mention that the higher fee a Mid Respectable could command would wipe out the reduction he was offering Flutirr. "There are no other Low Nobles nearby, your Nobleness. You can't get a better price."

"I am not going higher than seven."

"Seven and three-quarters."

He mulled over the choice and resisted a childish impulse to kick his left ankle with his right foot in frustration. It would look unNoblish and immature, and might also ruin his expensive dragon-leather boots. They were about twelve years older than he was, which made them practically family heirlooms. He didn't want to ruin them and deprive his future children. As for the Mid Respectable, he could always use his prerogative as a High Noble to grant Low Respectable wages. "All right, but don't pester me for more later. This is final. Now help me find a Mid Respectable."

"That's easy. There's one right over there." The Low Noble pointed across the street. "Third floor, I think. I'll go get her." He ran across the street in a very unNoblish manner—clearly a promoted Respectable, Flutirr thought scornfully. Then, even worse, he called up to the window when he should have gone in, or, preferably, sent a messenger. A few moments later, a woman in her forties or fifties, approaching middle age, appeared at the door. She was wearing a black blouse, a pair of red pants, and a long yellow necklace. Flutirr frowned, then caught himself. Calm. Smooth. Neutral, he told his face muscles. When the Low Noble and the woman came near, he said with reproach, "She is wearing the colors of a High Respectable."

"Yes, but she is also wearing the colors of a Mid Respectable, your Nobleness—yellow necklace, black blouse. The law says only that one wears the colors of one's class, not that they be dominant."

Flutirr paused. The lad was right, but he was still uneasy. "That may be so, but it is still imprudent of her to imply something that is not true."

"Should I ask her to go change, your Nobleness?"

At that moment, a clock somewhere stuck three. Already! He had to be home by five to get ready for dinner, and that was almost three miles away. "No. Do not bother. Let us depart, and I will pay her five Jublas." He began to walk swiftly without a backward glance until the boy called out from behind.

"Hey, slow down. We can't walk that fast." Flutirr stopped to wait, glaring at them down his long nose until they caught up. It was true that a Noble—particularly a High Noble—was not supposed to express any emotion whatsoever, irritation included. It was acceptable, however, to twitch the eyebrows and make a few slight changes in the stance to show annoyance at a lower-class Nelvin, as long as the purpose was intimidation and one did not go too far. He started walking again with exaggerated slowness, long legs straddling the ground, then he sped up until they reached a comfortable, respectable dozen feet or so from the Mid Tolerable.

"You, whatever your name is, go ask that Tolerable the meter and title of that song."

"You dragged me here to ask him *that?*" the boy asked indignantly.

"Yes. And I'm paying good money for this, so do as I say, or no pay."

Groaning like a Tolerable, the boy turned to the Mid Respectable and dutifully repeated the question. She walked over, spoke briefly with the Mid Tolerable, and returned.

"I am playing in 6/8 time, your Supreme Nobleness, and the song is a twenty-five-minute piece called 'Unicorns in the Forest,' " the Mid Respectable said, carefully addressing the Low Noble. He repeated everything to Flutirr, since it was illegal even to acknowledge that one had heard the words of a lower-class Nelvin.

"Who wrote it," Flutirr asked, and the procedure was repeated.

The answer: "I wrote 'Unicorns in the Forest' myself, in my youth." Flutirr raised his eyebrows, then lowered them to a more decent height.

"And why did he choose to use 6/8 time rather than the superior 2/4 or 4/4 time?"

The response: "Both 2/4 and 4/4 times were too slow for the mood I was searching for, your Nobleness. I wanted a light, playful mood alternating with the intensity of a unicorn fight, your Nobleness, and also I wanted—''

"That is sufficient. Ask him what he meant by mood. I was taught in school that the ideal to be striven for in playing music is mathematical precision, not sickening sentiment.''

The response: "Oh no, it is just the opposite, your Nobleness. A rhythm is important to give music its structure, but, not to be disrespectful, your Most Supreme High Nobleness, you need feelings too or the whole meaning of the music is lost.''

"This so-called meaning of his is in the mathematical beauty and precision of the piece, not in the feelings.''

The response: "Ah, but if you want mathematical beauty—not to be disrespectful of course, your Nobleness—couldn't you simply look at a math theorem? I realize, of course, your Highest Nobleness, that I am not well-educated and you know much more than me, but doesn't it seem more logical, your Nobleness, to look at math books when you want to enjoy math, and turn to music when you want to express yourself, and dig to the center of your soul and try to understand it? Where, your Supreme Nobleness, is the soul in numbers?''

"The soul in numbers,'' Flutirr sputtered, and caught himself. He mustn't let himself show anger. Take a deep breath, count to ten, and continue. "Look, if I want to *express* myself,'' he said, glaring down the point of his nose at the Low Noble, "then

I will—I'll—'' His mind drew an utter blank. Painting was out because it was too messy to be strongly encouraged among Nobles, and Nobles were required to use the same mathematical precision in painting that was used in music. Sculpting, sketching, and carving were out for the same reasons. Storytelling was illegal among Nobles. There was absolutely nothing he could refer to. "Well, what I am saying is, I can survive just fine without expressing myself the way he puts it,'' he said, almost stammering.

The message and response took an unbearably long time to be relayed. then the Mid Respectable returned and recited the response.

"Well, again, your Nobleness, I do not wish to be disrespectful, but it does seem to me, your Nobleness, that all Nelvins need to be able to express themselves. It isn't enough to know how to play the music, your Supreme Nobleness, you should be able to put some *feelings* in it too, or so it seems to me. I think it makes Nelvins go kind of sour and bitter inside if they don't think about themselves, because you have to think about yourself to play music the way I play it. It helps to play out all those bad feeling you have inside so you don't have to think about them anymore, and the good things too, your Supreme Nobleness, so you can feel like you are sharing something of yourself with the world. I know you know more than me about music, but that really is the way it seems to me, your Nobleness, and I do hope you don't see fit to report me, your Supreme High Nobleness, because

I don't mean to be disrespectful. I'm just saying what I think, your Nobleness.''

Flutirr frowned. ''Well—well—of course I still disagree, but look, I'm busy, I have things to get to, so here is your pay.'' He opened his money bag, then hesitated. ''Oh, but also, you don't supp—that is, I would like him to teach me just how he does that 6/8 thing, and I will pay him one Jubla for it.''

The message was relayed and the Mid Tolerable came within hearing distance, yet remained a respectable distance away. ''Why, certainly, your Most Supreme High Nobleness, of course I will be delighted to. It is really very simple, your Nobleness. You are familiar with eighth notes, I am sure?''

Almost before the relay was completed, Flutirr responded: ''As a matter of fact, I am not, since the only notes taught by my school are quarter notes or longer. Now stop this flattering and get to the point.''

The response: ''Well, you see, your Nobleness, a quarter note is made of two beats, an eighth note is made of one, and 6/8 time has six eighth notes to a measure, and that's all there is to it. See, it goes like this, your Nobleness.'' The old man demonstrated on the accordion, tapping the heel of his foot, causing the whole leg to waver, to dance on every beat. ''You see—very simple, your Supreme Nobleness.''

Flutirr frowned. The song was barbarous, the notes were clipped short, they trembled and weren't quite perfect, and—and he could almost see a unicorn in his mind's eye frolicking in the wind, lifting its silvery-ivory horn to the moonlight and stars. He

22

could feel a gentle breeze on his face crooning of green seas, and he felt his fingers reaching for the harp strings, but he stopped himself just in time. Better to keep his hands in his pockets, away from the harp, like a Respectable, than to let them trickle over the strings like a Tolerable. Curtly, he said, "Yes, this is all very interesting, but I must go now. Low Noble, this is your pay," and he handed him the bills and three coins. "Mid Respectable, your five Jublas," he said, addressing the Low Noble as custom dictated. "And Mid Tolerable, this is your pay for your assistance." He held himself stiffly, his toes curled inside his boots with tension, but neither the Low Noble nor the Mid Respectable discovered the small ten-Jubla note folded inside the single bill to be delivered to the Tolerable. His toes relaxed, and he walked away without a further word, since a High Noble should never thank his inferiors.

Before long, he came across the pastry stand again, and his eyes guiltily stole a glance at the wild nut pastries. He hadn't had any in almost a year, since no one else in his household liked them and the cooks rarely made them. He paused and pretended to study the books on the table next to the pastries, struggling to ignore the food and make himself go on. Instead he turned to the table and glared down his nose at the Mid Respectable. "One wild nut pastry and make it fast," he snapped. Her mouth gaped stupidly open.

"Your . . . your Nobleness, are you sure?" she said. He said nothing, but glared at her.

She hastily wrapped the spongy cake and handed

it to him. "For you, your High Nobleness, my price is a quarter-Jubla." He jerked his money bag open, tossed a quarter-Jubla piece rudely on the table, and gingerly took the pastry from her hand, careful not to touch her skin. "Thank you and good *day*," he snapped, and he turned sharply away.

Flutirr waited until he was a comfortable distance from the market square before unwrapping the pastry; after all, he couldn't let the lower-class citizens see a High Noble eating in public. As he folded back the thin paper, he whistled a few notes, and realized he was whistling a short passage from "Unicorns in the Forest." He bit his tongue to make himself stop, though a sore temptation urged him to continue. He looked with horror at the cake he had bought from the Mid Respectable. His hand trembled, and he wondered what his parents would say if they ever knew.

Chapter 2

IF Flutirr had been a Tolerable he would have groaned: Liz-Nirrr-Heen, the most exacting of all the Instructors of his class, was grading his group in music today. She always gave prompt and severe criticism of the barest quiver in a note, the slightest discrepancy from the correct answer in history or economics or any other subject. As a consequence, many of his yellow marks had come from her. Even Syner, the star pupil of the class, failed to escape completely her criticism.

The Music Instructor spoke. "The piece is 'Moonlight' by Kes-Herm-Lilitind. You will note it was written by a Low Noble and accordingly has numerous mathematical flaws. As I am sure you observed in practicing this piece over the past three weeks, it nevertheless has many strengths and is still worthy of our attention. When I give the signal you may begin." The Music Instructor lowered her hands, and the first musical notes piped into the air. Mere seconds into the song, Nirrr-Heen whipped out her dye-dart and squirted a small amount of thick yellow dye at the clothing of a nearby student for some minor error. They began a complicated section of the song, and Flutirr plucked one of the strings the wrong way, causing the note to be fainter than it should have been. Heen squirted him with two small discs of yellow dye then added a medium-sized disc equivalent to five of the smaller ones. *Curse* those irritating yellow marks, and curse Nirrr-Heen who gave them out so liberally, Flutirr almost muttered under his breath. A few yellow marks here and there might not be serious, but they could add up pretty quickly with someone like Heen wielding the dye-dart.

The first movement faded away and everyone paused a moment before continuing. The second movement was very simple, and Flutirr let his fingers do the work as his mind wandered—they seemed to know the piece better than he did. His fingers did a trick he would have found difficult a few years ago, and he gave himself a small mental compliment for it. He would never be the best in the class, but he was still a decent player. Compared to the Respectables and Tolerables downtown, he was even outstanding. The lower classes did not receive enough education to bring their music to the level of Nobles. Why waste money and time educating Nelvins who were going to do nothing more than sell products or make horseshoes for the rest of their lives? Who, in fact, were not capable of doing more than menial jobs?

Yet that Mid Tolerable he had heard the other day, the composer of that intriguing 'Unicorns in the Forest' piece, had played rather well. The unNoblishness of that dart! Two additional yellow marks, and he couldn't even remember how he had earned them, since his mind had been elsewhere. So, what had he been thinking about? Something about music? Oh yes, the composer of 'Unicorns in the Forest.' Yes, a nice piece, really, if you ignored the unNoblish 6/8 meter. On the other hand, once you thought about it, even the meter didn't seem too bad. Flutirr was inclined to forgive a few flaws for the emotional intensity of the piece, sickening sentiment and all, despite knowing it was an unNoblish thought. Now how *did* that piece go? He would hate to forget it, unNoblish or not. It was something like diddi *da*dadoda, or wasn't it more like diddi *dada-da*da? He might have forgotten the precise rhythm, but he still recalled the way it should be played on the harp, with *this* finger here, *that* finger there, then quickly pluck those stings before moving on to *this* string, then these strings—

On his left knee Flutirr felt the familiar warm damp feel of the dye. When he glanced at it he almost froze in déjà vu horror: it was not the yellow disc he had expected. It was gray. Another gray mark in his records. Seventeen years of no more than ordinary yellow marks from day to day turned instantly into a puff of dust. Only at that moment did Flutirr realize, to his even deeper shame and horror, that he had actually played the unNoblish notes he had been trying to remember. Even the grossly inefficient hearing of a Human could have detected that horrible error. What in Nobleness's name would his parents say? They would know by that evening, since parents were told on the very day a gray mark was issued. There would be no four-day respite for Flutirr until the time of the Weekly Report.

And even worse—how would his peers react? His classmates had not spoken to him for more than a year after his first gray mark. Even when they did begin interacting with him again, the conversation had been superficial, and the friendly overtures rare. Perhaps he could have salvaged a few friendships then— but by that time, Flutirr was already lost. He was lost in the muddle of the day-to-day gossip he had missed over the previous year. He was lost in the complexities of the group dynamics that had evolved without him in it. After suffering his classmates' silent treatment for so long, he no longer knew how to respond to the most casual remark. The magical skill his peers seemed to have of grabbing a conversation and infusing it with cleverness, wit, and entertainment was forever out of his reach.

To this day, only Violirrr—who had moved to the district of Trilene at the age of eleven, and thus had no memory of Flutirr's first gray mark—had ever been a true friend. If it took seventeen years to forgive one gray mark, then how long would it take for his peers to forgive a second?

The third movement began and was mercifully short. Flutirr put his harp by his chair and waited while Nirrr-Heen took the place of the Music Instructor on the podium. "You may stand," she ordered, and the class stood. "Remove your discs and approach me when your name is called." Flutirr leaned to peel away the yellow and gray discs that had firmed into a rubbery substance. Clutching them in his hand, he concentrated on keeping his knees and hands still, rather than trembling as they were trying to do. The monotonous voice droned through the names in alphabetical order. Flutirr distractedly studied the clouds drifting near the horizon until the first of the "S" students was called, and the names began to emerge into Flutirr's awareness.

"Sheenhill."

"Seven yellow marks."

"Sillayteen."

"Four yellow marks."

"Tersylli."

"Zero yellow marks."

"Willyahe."

"Eight yellow marks."

She had missed his name! Flutirr almost interrupted the proceedings to point out the error, but then he understood. She must be saving him for last. Then she would probably do the same thing that had been done to him seventeen years ago. Oh, Dearest Nobleness—the discs in Flutirr's hand became sticky from the sweat of his hand. Curse that unNoblish Mid Tolerable and his disgusting song that had brought him to this trouble in the first place. If he had never heard that barbarous piece he would never have made such an unNoblish error in such a simple passage of that song. The list wound to its end, and at long last he was called. Careful not to move too quickly or too slowly, he approached the podium, eyes resting respectfully on Nirrr-Heen's face.

"Nine yellow marks. One gray mark."

In a neat precise hand, Heen recorded the numbers in Flutirr's records. Then the same hand riffled through the papers in the folder and halted at his master sheet. "I see this is not your first gray mark, Flutirr."

"Yes, Noble Heen."

"At age six. For grossly unNoblish behavior. I am not surprised you were punished in this manner."

"Yes, Nirrr-Heen."

"This gives you a total of two Black Marks, seven gray marks, and a little over three thousand yellow marks. That means you are two gray marks and two thousand yellow marks away from your third Black Mark, Flutirr."

That close! He had known from his weekly and annual reports that he was accumulating many penalty marks over the years, but he had always been too afraid to check his precise total. There was still a good chance of his finishing school without actually reaching that third Black Mark, but he would have to be careful never again to make a mistake like the one he had made today. "Yes, Noble Heen."

Heen faced one of the students and ordered sharply: "Sillayteen. Bring Flutirr his harp." The harp was brought to him.

"Flutirr, play 'Moonlight' in Ultimate Perfection. If you succeed, your gray mark will be erased."

Ultimate Perfection! This was a state of Perfection only Expert Professionals could regularly achieve, not at all like the playing expected of students. He could never do it, yet he had to try. He put the strap over his shoulder and began to play. The first few meters were flawless. Even that complicated section that had given him his first seven yellow marks went well. But then one of the strings trembled in the wrong way. The tremble was only barely detectable by Nelvin hearing; no one of any other race of Trillilani—not even an Elvin—would have heard it at all. It would never had earned him even one yellow mark in class. It did, however, detract from the Ultimate Perfection he had been striving for. He had failed.

"Thank you, Flutirr. That will be all."

All? Did that mean she was not going to—but he was not dismissed yet—

"Flutirr, put down your harp and come forward."

Stiffly, Flutirr put down the harp. Felling a mite dizzy when he rose again, he stepped forward. She was going to do it after all.

Nirr-Heen spat in his face, in each eye. This time,

at least, no one laughed. That would have been unNoblish.

"You may sit, Flutirr."

Flutirr picked up his harp, walked to his seat, and sat. He let the spit dry on his face as the next lesson began.

Chapter 3

NEVER before had Flutirr been here at night. Always before, he had arrived in bright sunlight right after school. The light seemed to expiate his unNoblish actions, as if he were saying to some imaginary witness, See, I'm not doing anything wrong, I have nothing to hide and that's why I'm here in the daylight. Now that it was dark, however, his visit to this district seemed more illegal, more wrong. Because of this he had spent the first few sleepless hours of the night debating with his temptation to return. There were no excuses to be made to himself for coming at night. No wild nut pastry to be bought, no errand to be done at night. There could be only further corruption.

Yet temptation had won. His soul had been wounded that morning and he needed some kind of salve for his spirit that couldn't be found near his home. Perhaps all he sought, he told himself, was to know he was not as inferior as he had been made to feel that day. Perhaps all he needed was to see the lower classes, to see that he was better than they; then he could go home and sleep. He was after all more Noblish than they could ever be. Their every gesture was coarse—for that matter, that they gestured at all was an unNoblish thing; their clothing, their laughter, their tears, their music were all unNoblish.

Apparently even the Respectables and Tolerables of the district were fairly well-to-do since the lights on this street were many, and they truly lit the way—not like the sparse lights in poorer areas that were too dim to be useful. During his visits here, Flutirr had noticed many tables with nut products. This was probably what accounted for the wealth in this area, since nuts were a major food staple among Nelvins.

The lights seemed to have a reddish cast, giving the bare market tables an odd gloss, like ghostly memories of generations of Nelvin barter and trade. And here, centered between two lights, was the pastry stand. In the shadows, it seemed for a moment that the Mid Respectable was still behind the table, waiting for a customer to sell to. When Flutirr passed, however, there was nothing but darkness.

Flutirr halted and half leaned, half sat, on the pastry-stand table. The sound of the bell startled him, then he braced himself for the next clang that never came. It was 1 A.M. then. He had never, to his recollection, been out this late before; this visit, more than any other, would enrage his parents if they knew. For the first time, Flutirr felt fear. Before what had happened that day, he had never really thought of the inevitable consequences of his unNoblish actions. In some vague way, he had assumed his parents would be angry for a time, then would recover enough to prevent or minimize any demotion that threatened.

Now, with the gray mark he had earned that day, that would no longer be true. One gray mark could be tolerated. His parents had been angry, of course, at his first gray mark, but it was only the usual anger of any parent at a naughty child. It was rare to earn a gray mark, but it was not as though Flutirr was the only Nelvin to accomplish it; a handful of Flutirr's own relatives and ancestors had earned gray marks too. Even his illustrious Great-great-grand-uncle Flutirrillly, President of the High Council, after whom Flutirr had been named, had earned a gray mark during his teens. Two gray marks, however, was a dragon of a different scale. No one in the Till line had ever earned two gray marks. It had been serious enough for both his parents to be called in the middle of their Council meeting, and they had been waiting for him when he came home. There had been an awkward moment of silence: angry silence on his parents' side, frightened silence on his. Then his father had spoken first.

"We have just heard of your gray mark, Flutirr."

"Yes, Father," Flutirr had replied.

"I hope you realize the seriousness of this matter, Flutirr."

"I do, Noble Father."

"No ancestor of ours has ever earned more than one gray mark at once during his school years, Flutirr. In fact, the average total for a Till at the end of his schooling is only a little over two Black Marks, which you have well surpassed even without your two gray marks, Flutirr.''

"I am aware of that, Noble Father.'' At this moment, he had glanced at his father's right hand held stiffly by his side. Just as he had feared, the sixth finger was twitching in anger. Only the severest loss of temper could provoke his father enough to allow his tight self-control to slip in this way. Flutirr had inherited that same quirk, only it was the finger of his left hand that twitched and not his right. As a child, he had seriously considered amputating this errant finger, this evil part of his body that refused to bend to the self-control required of a High Noble. Then he had taken a closer observation of other Nobles and discovered he was not alone. Others had a tic in their eye when they were embarrassed, or their cheek muscles jerked when they were afraid.

"Didn't you practice, Flutirr?''

"Yes, Noble Father!''

"Then why?''

Flutirr's lips parted for a second, fumbling for words, an explanation that could somehow excuse his behavior. Finally, he could say only "I don't know.''

"Flutirr!''

Flutirr almost flinched. His father had actually barked at him. He was angrier than he had ever seen him before.

"Flutirr. Flutirr, your mother and I had a long discussion before you came home. We have come to the decision that we may have to consider Disownment, Flutirr.''

He was barely able to push out the words: "Y-yes, Noble Father.'' Even Partial Disownment was a serious matter, since he would be automatically demoted to Low Noble class. It was possible to appeal to the Councils and wrest a re-promotion to High Noble class, but even then he would be considered a first-generation High Noble—ten generations too young to have a seat on even the lowest of Councils. Partial demotion would most likely mean poverty for the rest of Flutirr's one-hundred-plus years of life.

"At first we thought of Disowning you immediately. We have decided, however, to give you one more chance, Flutirr. One.''

"Yes, Noble Father.''

"One more gray mark, Flutirr, or even half or one-quarter of a gray mark, or one instance of grossly unNoblish behavior, and we may Disown you. We are not discussing Partial Disownment, Flutirr. We are discussing Total Disownment.''

"I understand, Noble Father.'' Total Disownment—almost nothing worse than that could possibly happen to him. He could be demoted to Tolerable class without even the right to appeal the demotion.

"I hope so, Flutirr. Go wash for lunch.''

So why was he even here? Flutirr asked himself once again. It was even more dangerous than it previously had been to be here, especially at night. If it were day, he could find a myriad of excuses for being here that, as long as his more explicitly illegal actions went undiscovered, might have convinced his parents to consider only Partial Disownment rather than Total Disownment. At night, there were no excuses. He should be heading home instead of dawdling at the table of a Mid Respectable. Instead, he stood and continued down the road. He walked empty of thought, letting his feet take him wherever they desired. Buildings became fewer and fewer, lights became farther and farther apart, but Flutirr noticed this only in an absentminded manner, until he wandered a few paces past a dim light and suddenly realized there was no other light nearby, and he did not know quite where he was. Then he took a deep breath and looked up at the sky.

It was full of stars.

Startled, Flutirr stared. He had, of course, seen pictures in the science books at school, and had caught glimpses of stars near his home before. He had just never realized how many stars could be in one sky once the bright streetlights were taken away, and the moons had never seemed this bright in the city. If only all three moons were out tonight, that would be an even more beautiful sight! Unfortunately, that third moon was hiding its face elsewhere that night. Forgetting all about time, Flutirr walked onward, looking at the sky, and almost stumbled into the river. When he had pulled himself to his feet again, he looked up and saw a fire across the river.

Curious, he walked closer. Squinting revealed vague outlines of gray huts in the background and clusters of Nelvins around the fire, hunching on the ground in silence. Then Flutirr heard a booming voice:

"This following tale is, I do believe, seven centuries old. It took place over a thousand years ago in an Elvin land to the west. Now, this is another one of my long-spun adventure tales, so if any of you want to save y'allselves from the torture, y'all perfectly welcome to sneak away to your comfy mattresses now, and I won't do any more than whip you twenty lashes every day for a week." A murmur of laughter wafted across the brook, and no one moved.

It was obviously a storytelling circle, probably a group of Tolerables, since they were the only classes allowed to tell fictional tales. The voice began again: "In this Elvin land, there was a young lad by the name of Duucaniel who fell in love with a lass with long red hair, for as you all know there are some Elvins with odd-colored hair. Now, this lass was rather plain-looking as Elvins go, but she had the sweetest character anywhere and painted the most beautifulest pictures you ever saw, so every lad in the village wished to be her mate—" A wind started to blow toward the fire, against Flutirr's back. The storyteller paused a moment to let his audience move away from the billowing smoke.

If Flutirr were caught listening to this tale, he would be demoted with or without Disownment. He had money, but not nearly enough to bribe all the Council members it would take to ease his demotion. Besides, this was such a serious crime the Council members would be reluctant to let it pass for any sum. It was time to go home anyway. The Nelvins moved near the fire as they avoided the smoke. The light flickered over their clothes in random waves, and a rainbow of colors disclosed itself in the form of rags and patches and worn clothing. Flutirr swallowed a gasp. This was even more reason he should leave this instant. Only classless ones—having no legal existence, and therefore no colors of their own—could wear such a myriad of colors.

Then the voice began again: "So, as I was saying, every lad in the village wished to be her mate, 'cept for a few that found other girls to like. This little lass, however, vowed to love only the bravest boy in all the village—" There was something about that voice that kept Flutirr at his spot. The Nelvin was clearly uneducated, yet his voice seemed to hold magic within it. Perhaps it was cadence, or perhaps it had something to do with the subtle power that carried the voice despite the gentle tremor of old age. Whatever it was that fascinated him, Flutirr hesitated to leave. Instead, he stepped a little closer to the bank in order to hear more clearly. ". . . The lad of our tale was, as any young fellow would be, mightily depressed at the conditions, but he went up to that attic of his—"

What was this here under his hands? Flutirr squinted and eventually made out the vague outlines of a bridge. What he had discovered was one of its posts. So this was how they crossed the river. Brook. Whatever. He leaned on the post to take a little weight off his feet. ". . . but of course it was mightily dusty from all that time up there, so Duucaniel got out his cloth and cleaned it off best he could. The sword became quite shiny with a remarkably sharp edge and quite useful—not at all like those showy swords of our Nobles around here!" The audience laughed, and Flutirr stiffened, his chin lifting high. The classless storyteller had no right to call his sword useless! He would concede that Noble swords were more for show than defense, and it was rare for a Noble to bother learning how to use his or her sword. Still it *was* used—at least to command respect—

Flutirr hated to admit it, but the truth was, the classless one was right. The swords were little more than symbols of rank, just like the cape and fancy boots, and the blue and purple colors. ". . . Off he went to find that nasty fire-breathing dragon—" Fire-breathing dragon? This was complete nonsense; every Nelvin knew dragons breathed a poisonous gas, not fire. Nevertheless, the story was fascinating, and worth ignoring a few petty inaccuracies. ". . . After riding for a long day, he crawled into the bushes alongside the path and slept the night away except for when some pesky bugs came along and bit the poor lad. When he woke he was as itchy as crazy, but kept going on riding and riding and riding through the forest . . ."

Flutirr's skin twitched and his heart sped from the anxiety that urged him to leave this unNoblish tale— yet he remained. The story wound to its end: Duucaniel was killed by the dragon, but his spirit left his body and returned to the village. There he found that his true love had committed suicide upon hearing of his death, for she had loved only him all along. The two spirits lived together in the village and theoretically lived there still. Well, there were irritating inaccuracies in the tale, but he had enjoyed it. The fire-breathing dragon had been more exciting and dangerous than one that breathed only poison. Flutirr could never have identified with anyone who could kill a dragon single-handedly, so it seemed right that Duucaniel had been killed. On the other hand, it would have been disappointing to end the story there, with Duucaniel never attaining his wished-for mate. So, it was a very pleasing tale even if it could never possibly occur.

Flutirr wondered what time it was—probably close to three or even four in the morning. He was not expected for breakfast until about six-thirty, and he was already dressed, so he was still safe. He hesitated—though he did not know why—until the Nelvins put out the fire and returned to their huts. Then when he was about to leave, a few scattered classless ones with lanterns left their huts and headed for the bridge. Quickly, Flutirr hid behind the posts as they crossed.

"Hey, Reffie, I hear your little girl started walking yesterday, that right?" one classless one called to another.

"Yup, that's right. Two big steps! Before you know it, she'll be ready to pick nuts and earn her food."

There was a brief pause, then in a soft voice the other said: "My youngest boy has . . . a new job."

"I thought he was delivering messages for that Low Tolerable messenger?"

"This job pays better." A Human would not have heard his whisper.

"Oh? Is it a Mid Tolerable employer then?"

The only sound was the sound of breathing, and the sound of more feet clattering over the bridge. Then suddenly one of the Nelvins stopped and swung his lantern almost directly in the face of the other. The other Nelvin stopped. Nelvins beginning to pass them slowed down to hear.

"Good High Nobleness's sakes, Kipper, you didn't send him *there*, did you? Is *that* where he's been the past two days?"

"I have seven other children to worry about too, Reffie, and now that my mother's too ill to work that's even less food coming in for us."

"But in Cursed Nobleness's name, Kipper, he could *die* there—how could you do that to him?"

"There was nothing else I could do, Reffie." The other classless ones clustered around the pair.

"Oh, Damnable Nobleness's sakes, Kipper, there's always something—"

"There isn't, and you damn well know it."

There was a pause. "I'm sorry. I got upset. What medicine are they testing on him?"

"Anti-Sporadasm shots."

For a moment, everyone was hushed. Sporadasm was one of the most painful, serious diseases known to Nelvins. Another Nelvin spoke. "That's what my husband was given and tested with a year ago." The Nelvins pressed closer, the better to lend a hand of sympathy.

"That's how my child died three years ago at the Medicine-Testing Center," another voice added softly.

"With my child they tested the smallpox."

The murmuring faded away, and Kipper spoke again. "Perhaps this time the medicine will work, and my boy will live." Feebly the Nelvins tried to comfort him. A few stories were told of Nelvins who had reputedly gone to Medicine-Testing Centers and survived—a neighbor of a cousin in the district of L'han, the old woman with those pretty white flowers in front of her hut. One of the Nelvins interrupted.

"I'm sorry, Kipper. It's getting time to be heading into the city."

The Nelvins' weary footsteps trickled away, then more streamed across the bridge. When the stars began to blur into purple streaks and a weak glow peered over the horizon, one more Nelvin came. He did not cross the bridge, but sat under it. A moment later, the sounds of a flute drifted across the river. This was the time for Flutirr to go; he had perhaps an hour and a half to spare and he needed an hour of it to walk home. But then the music enraptured him.

It was the most beautiful music Flutirr had ever heard. Somewhere in the deep shadowy corners of his mind, he knew that no other High Noble would ever accept such a piece, and just a few weeks ago he himself would have been disgusted by it. But he had changed. He no longer cared so much about petty mathematical definitions of music. They were pointless, they made no sense, they had nothing to do with what music really was or what it could be in the hands of someone like that Mid Tolerable he had heard, or like this boy. Wearily, Flutirr closed his eyes, and the music swept over him, making him dizzy, or perhaps he was only tired.

At first he merely sat, swaying in time to the music. Then he had the insight that the music was a celebration of the sun. He could not explain how he had reached that feeling; it had come unbidden to him. Something about the music suggested it to him. This piece far surpassed any of the Noblish songs he had played in school on either harp or flute. It caused an ache in him, a tingling in his fingers, and he very sorely wished he could play along with this Nelvin.

The song faded away, and Flutirr opened his eyes to see the sun completely above the horizon. As Flutirr stood, the classless Nelvin crossed the bridge. Flutirr could see now why he had not joined the others in their walk to work: one of his legs was shorter than the other and his mouth was disfigured. He walked too slowly to carry messages quickly, and it was possible he did not even speak. Not even a Low Tolerable would want such a crippled figure as his employee. The only job this classless Nelvin could possibly do was beg. The Nelvin glanced in Flutirr's direction. Flutirr froze—he must not see him, he must not see him, he mustn't—

It was too late. He had been seen. The pair, the High Noble and the classless Nelvin, stared at each other, equally startled, until the classless one turned away and limped down the path.

Chapter 4

TRYING to look inconspicuous, Flutirr loitered about across the street from the Medicine-Testing Center, thinking. The Center was an immense building, yet it was said to be used only to test medicines on tiny rats. It had never before occurred to Flutirr to question this contradiction. He had never even considered the possibility that the Medicine experimenters would experiment on Nelvins unless they had already contracted a disease the Medicine Experimenters were trying to defeat. These were, after all, mostly Nobles. Nobles, by definition, were noble—too noble to knowingly infect healthy Nelvins with fatal diseases just to test a medicine. Such a practice was the equivalent of murder. It was unthinkable to suspect these noble Nobles of such a crime.

Yet he had heard those classless Nelvins. And how else to explain the need for so much space at the Medicine-Testing Center? These Nelvins needed a place to stay until the experimental medicine worked, or failed to work. A Nelvin ravaged with Sporadasm disease, or any other illness, could hardly be expected to walk a three-hour round trip to and from his grisly job. Flutirr could no longer deny the truth to himself: these Nobles he had always looked up to during his childhood almost as much as he looked up to the council members of Trilene, the Nelvins who had once saved his own life from disease with one of the medicines they had discovered, these Nobles were murderers.

No! His mind balked once more at the idea. It was wrong to call their practices murder when they were only trying to find the best medicines for diseases that threatened the lives of every Nelvin. Some sacrifice of life was necessary in order to save even more lives.

Even this logic failed to convince Flutirr. Was it truly justified to fritter away Nelvin lives when pesky vermin were available everywhere for the same purpose? These rats would certainly suffer too, but no more than if they were caught in a painful trap in some Nelvin household. And there were also plenty of Nelvins already diseased to experiment on. It was cruel to allow what must be hundreds of Nelvins to die in this way.

Except—these Nelvins had no class. It was actually a benefit to Nelvin society to eliminate these disgusting individuals who were the descendants of Nelvins who had committed crimes so horrible they had been stripped of class and legal existence. That made them lower than a flea on a rat, Flutirr thought to himself. Surely this fact was undebatable. If a Nelvin did not exist he could not be murdered. These Medical Experimenters were, therefore, no murderers.

But what flea on a rat could cast the eerie spell of that song by the classless Nelvin?

What flea on a rat could tell a tale like that elderly Nelvin last night?

What creature lower than a flea on a rat ever cared enough for another Nelvin to try to comfort him in his pain?

What abominable thing could mourn for the near-certain death of his son, the pain evident in every gesture, the sorrow making his voice tremble? And it took a strong spirit not only to survive what Kipper was going through now but also to drag himself to the city to work day after day just as though his son were not going to die.

Yes, that Kipper showed every bit as much courage as a High Noble. His decision to send his own son to the Center was certainly a brutal decision, but it must have been the hardest decision of Kipper's life. The pain in his voice said that it had not been a thought-less decision. This was a Nelvin who had feelings just as Flutirr and every other Noble had feelings, even if they would never deign to reveal them. How could such a Nelvin be considered so worthless his existence was not even recognized?

Yet he had sent his own son to die.

Flutirr took one last look at the building where a Nelvin who did not exist had sent a little boy who did not exist to die.

Restlessly, Flutirr began to walk. He was almost at

the heterogeneous district before he noted the direction he was headed in. His steps slowed at the realization then sped up again. One last visit would not hurt, he almost murmured aloud to himself.

Once again Flutirr saw the pastry stand, and once again he started to pass by but turned around and went back.

"One wild nut pastry," Flutirr said.

"Yes, your Nobleness," the Mid Respectable said quietly, as she wearily wrapped the pastry. Flutirr took a quarter-Jubla piece from his purse, but hesitated. For the first time he looked more closely at the Mid Respectable. She was middle-aged, perhaps fifty or sixty at the youngest, and her skin stretched tight over her bones, seeming to harbor no flesh in between. It was the boniness of near-starvation. Even the exotic wild nut pastries, her most expensive sales item, apparently did not earn enough for her to feed herself adequately. Flutirr suddenly realized that he had made a small contribution to her state: normally wild nut pastries cost more than the quarter-Jubla he had paid her in the past.

"Respectable, a quarter-Jubla is not the normal price you charge, is it?" he said stiffly, editing all concern from his voice.

"Well, your Nobleness, I would not ask you to pay more than—"

"What do you usually charge?"

"Three-quarters of a Jubla, or sometimes seven-eighths for particularly good quality like these. But of course you don't need to—"

"Quite all right," he said, and drew an additional five-eighths of a Jubla from his purse. He handed the money to the Mid Respectable. For the first time their skin brushed together, and Flutirr did not flinch. "Thank you and good day," he added, his tone not quite as rude as before. He turned, and went home.

Chapter 5

FLUTIRR stood and hung his flute on his belt. The new song they were practicing for school was supposed to be easier on the harp than the flute, but he had chosen to use the latter this time to keep his flute-playing skills sharp. He brought his chair to the storehouse. As he started to leave, one of his classmates called out to him.

"Flutirr, have you made plans for the afternoon?"

Startled, for he had not expected anyone to speak to him so soon after his second gray mark, Flutirr said, "No, I have not."

"I am having a few classmates at my house for a music-sharing, and perhaps we will practice the new song. Would you like to come, Flutirr?"

Flutirr almost refused the invitation, because he had earned twenty-two yellow marks that day on the history and the economics exams and he wanted to study for the math exam the following day to make sure he earned no more. Then Flutirr reasoned to himself that it was rare that he received a social invitation, and if he turned this one down he might not get another for a long time.

"I may come for a brief time. I have to study for the math exam."

"Of course. You know where my house is located?"

"I am familiar with it, thank you."

"That is good. I will see you at three."

"At three." The students departed without a further word.

Flutirr reached the doorstep, looked for the knocker and found none. Then he saw the bellrope to the side of the door and tugged on that. Sounds of someone bustling about came from inside, and a Mid Noble servant soon answered the door. Tillune's family was apparently wealthier than Flutirr had realized, to be able to afford a Mid Noble for a mere music-sharing. Mid Nobles always charged extravagant rates, and were strictly for one time occasions; Flutirr's own family had a Low Noble servant in permanent employ, but even that was rare. Both his parents were officers on the High Council, and could afford it.

"How may I help you, your Nobleness?" said the Mid Noble.

"I am here to see the young Sillayteen."

"Right this way please, your Nobleness."

Flutirr followed the servant, and waited as she opened the parlor doors.

"Your friends are here, your Nobleness."

Tillune-Lilll-Sillayteen stood and nodded in Flutirr's direction. "Welcome, honorable one," he said in the manner every Nelvin addressed his or her guests. "We were about to listen to Tilny play on her oboe."

"Then I have arrived just in time," Flutirr said. He sat and nervously leaned his flute upright against his chair. Cursed Nobleness, he thought to himself—he should have come earlier, to avoid the awkwardness of being a latecomer. He tried to compose himself, and desperately tried to think of a way to ease the clumsiness, but Tilny's music saved him from embarrassing himself. Flutirr leaned back in his chair and closed his eyes in an attempt to appreciate the music. Tilny was an excellent musician by High Noble standards, and rarely earned even a single yellow mark during Music Tests. It was expected that someday soon she would achieve Ultimate Perfection and become a Professional Musician. Nevertheless it was difficult to force his thinking into mathematical terms again after hearing the free-flowing music of the classless youth.

Yes, that was something he had to watch there—he must never listen to so much of the lower-class and classless music that he actually came to hate the music of the upper classes. With every visit among the lower classes, it was becoming more difficult to tear himself away, and more difficult to resist the temptation to return. Why, there was a time just two or three years ago when he would never have thought of going at all! Now, he had to expose himself to as much High Noble music as possible to learn to appreciate it again, or he would become irreversibly corrupted. He hardly dared imagine what such a corrupted Nelvin on the High Council could do to society.

The music faded away, and immediately a busy conversation began. Flutirr opened his eyes in panic. He had been planning to open the after-music conversation in order to make up for his awkward entrance, but now he was too late. He would have to try to squeeze in a few words later. He listened carefully for a break in the conversation but found none. At first everyone was commenting on Tilny's music, but before Flutirr could think of anything to add, they somehow started talking about school and their instructors and tests and homework. Then suddenly another student had agreed to play a piece on his accordion and the music began.

This time Flutirr did not even try to concentrate on the music. It was imperative that he contribute to the conversation, or it would be mutually agreed among his peers that he was not worth having as a guest again. He needed numerous acquaintances if he were to gain power on the High Council for himself and future generations of the Till line. And acquaintances were something he hadn't been attracting during his school years. He had to put all thought of the lower classes out of his mind and concentrate on making up for all the years of socialization he had missed. Now that he had two gray marks on his record, it was more vital than ever that he make contacts who could become potential supporters later.

So, what had the last topic of conversation been? Oh yes, about that controversial bill currently before the High Council that would permit very young Nelvin children to, in emergency situations, speak with those more than three classes above or below them. Nelvin children were always granted extraordinary independence and mobility; normally this was quite safe, as it was deeply ingrained in every Nelvin adult to keep a wary eye on any roaming child he or she saw, and it was unheard of to harm any of these vessels of society's future. Some Council members, however, had recently expressed concern that limitations on interclass communication caused a potential danger when a young child got into trouble and had only prohibited classes to appeal to for help. Tillune had argued against easing interclass-communication restrictions for children, claiming that a sufficient number of Nelvins were willing to bend the laws as appropriate to make such a ruling unnecessary. Well, Flutirr happened to disagree with his view, and right after the music ended was good time to continue the discussion. Now that he had determined his topic of conversation, he was able to turn his attention to the music to be ready for the end of the song.

The end came in a flurry of notes. Hastily, Flutirr inserted his thoughts before anyone else could begin to speak. "As I was about to say before this lovely, mathematically pure piece of Willyt's, I think that it is about time young children were permitted to communicate with a wider range of Nelvins when their own safety is in question—" He paused briefly, expecting Tillune to nod in acknowledgment so he could continue. Tillune sent a Noblishly tight, condescending smile. Discomfited, Flutirr blundered through the rest of his argument. "After all, even a Tolerable child carries the seeds of the future. Is it justified to allow any child to suffer the slightest risk to his or her safety because of the least inhibition against communication across class barriers? No, it is unreasonable—" The last few words trailed into silence when he saw the faces of his classmates. A Respectable or Tolerable would have seen nothing in their faces. Flutirr, as a High Noble, was sensitive to the least nuance in body language. Every face had the patronizing look of one who is watching someone make a faux pas in the secure knowledge that he, of course, would never make the same error.

How could he have been such an unNoblish idiot? The convention was to allow everyone a chance to make comments on the music before going on to the other topics. But he, blundering corrupted ignoramus that he was, had forgotten all about that and embarrassed himself in front of everyone. Someone said something he didn't hear, then the conversation was continued in the proper way. Music began again, and this time Flutirr kept silent when it ended. The other Nelvins commented on the music, then on the composer, then on other composers and other musicians. Before Flutirr could add a comment, the chatter came to a halt. Tillune faced Flutirr.

"Would you like to play a piece for us, Flutirr?"

Flutirr reached for his flute. "Certainly, Tillune. What would you like to hear?"

"I have recently become fond of 'Moonlight,' by Kes-Herm-Lilitind."

Nobles must never laugh, but Flutirr, with his sensitivity heightened by his peers' reaction to his faux pas, saw a mocking snigger behind every slightly-upturned corner of every lip in the room. Now Flutirr knew the real reason why he had been invited that day. It was not because anyone wanted his company or expected him to contribute to the conversation. It was not because anyone wanted to get to know him better or be a friend. He was here as a freak exhibit. See Flutirr humiliate himself all over again with the same piece that gave him so much trouble before. See the High Noble who has earned not one but two gray marks in his lifetime. See the High Noble struggle with a piece even a Respectable would find easy to play. See the High Noble who is so corrupted he deserves to be spat upon.

"Of course, I have not practiced the piece on flute. I would do better with harp." He considered suggesting a different piece, but held back. Everyone in the room knew Flutirr did not want to play that piece, and that he knew they knew it. They would only label him an unNoblish coward if he made too unsubtle an attempt to avoid the ordeal.

"You are welcome to borrow my harp, Flutirr."

He was trapped. There was no way to refuse. He took the harp as it was passed to him and stalled a moment tuning it before starting to play with his tremulous fingers. He must not fail, he must show the faintly mocking faces that he could indeed be a proper High Noble, that he deserved to be born to his station in life. His twelve fingers danced over the strings with a skill that would have been envied by the greatest of musicians among nearly any race. Yet Flutirr heard discords no creature besides a Nelvin would have heard, and he knew his playing was just barely a match for the average High Noble Nelvin. If he wanted to impress his classmates, some of whom would soon be his colleagues on the Low Council, he had to do better. Flutirr closed his eyes and thought of nothing but his fingers and the strings of his harp and what notes he must pluck next. The end of the first movement came before he knew it, and he paused the customary one and three-quarters of a second before beginning the next movement.

This was the movement he had failed at so utterly before. It was a simple one, there was no reason for him to fail a second time as long as he cleared his mind of every thought except the music. Yet all of a sudden it became more important than ever to play the best he had ever played in his life—not just to impress his peers, but simply because he knew he could never bear the knowledge that he had failed once again with the same piece he had mutilated before. It would be like admitting there was something wrong with him, some defect that kept him from being as Noblish as a High Noble should be. His fingers stiffened with his sudden anxiety. What if something went wrong, what if a finger slipped? The second movement was the easiest of the three to play, but it was even more agony than the first. It was a relief to complete the movement and go on to the third.

The performance hardly would have been judged as Ultimate Perfection, but both the second and third movements went more smoothly than Flutirr had expected they would. He had played better than usual. He opened his eyes and glanced around the room. For a moment there was silence, and Flutirr knew that behind every frozen face was a thwarted smirk.

"That was nicely played, Flutirr."

"Yes, that was very mathematically precise."

"The meter was well-timed."

Flutirr joined the polite charade, acknowledging each compliment. He returned the harp and sat back to listen to the conversation until it sludged its way to the end, with everyone making feeble excuses about other things to get to. Flutirr made his own excuse (he did have studying to do) and left. As he started walking down the path to the front gate, he heard the door open and swing shut behind him. He turned and saw his only friend, Violirrr, coming down the stairs. Hoping to salvage something from the wasted afternoon, Flutirr called out to him.

"Violirrr! I believe we have some fresh southern nuts—I could ask the cook to put them in a sauce if you would like to come for supper tomorrow night." A dinner invitation among Nelvins was extended only to friends, or to those whom you wished were your friends.

"I am afraid I cannot do that, Flutirr."

"If you are busy tomorrow, there is always next week."

With a queer emphasis, Violirrr repeated: "I am afraid I cannot do that, Flutirr," and it took Flutirr a second to realize that he didn't just mean tomorrow or next week, but ever.

"See you in school tomorrow," Flutirr said, just as though everything were still normal, and he didn't have two gray marks, and he were still friends with Violirrr.

He went down the path and through the gate and went home.

Chapter 6

WHEN Flutirr went downtown three days after the music-sharing, the Mid Respectable was not there with her pastries; it was late and many of the stands were closing. He would have to come earlier, Flutirr told himself, if he wanted to buy himself a late-night snack. Then again, he wasn't ever going to come here again. Such speculation was, therefore, pointless.

All three moons were out tonight: two crescents and one near-circle. The shimmering moons gave him enough light to find his way to the river and the bridge. Across the river he saw a flickering fire but only a few scattered Nelvins. He sat cross-legged at the foot of the bridge to doze. He woke a few times, due to a lingering swarm of bothersome bugs; when thus disturbed, the weary Flutirr only shifted his position and slept again. In time a commotion woke him. At first he squinted upward with bleary eyes, but then he pinpointed the sound and looked across the bridge.

There he saw the glaring fire and leaping and spinning around it were two classless Nelvins adorned with an incredible array of colored ribbons. Once Flutirr was awake enough to squeeze a coherent thought through his sluggish brain, he concluded that this must be the classless version of dancing. There was only one dance allowed to Nobles, and that was, as all other Noblish things, based on mathematical principles. The steps for this Noblish dance were neat, precise, and painfully slow, to prevent dancers from embarrassing themselves by making mistakes because the dance was too swift for them. Flutirr had always vaguely assumed that the dances of all classes were somewhat like the one he danced at weddings and ceremonies. Now he saw that he had been wrong. Both music and dance were complex; the feet and ribbons seemed to be only a blur of colors. Hands seemed to touch the ground almost as frequently as feet. The ribbons, he soon saw, were not merely decoration but were worn to be integrated into the dance itself: some steps appeared to have been contrived purely to show off the flowing ribbons, making them seem to perform a dance of their own.

After a few moments, another pair of Nelvins with a similar set of ribbons began to dance, and the first pair dissolved into the circle around the fire. Unable to see clearly, Flutirr took a few steps across the bridge and leaned over the railing to take a closer look at the illuminated space between the fire and the circle of Nelvins. Now he could see each step with greater clarity—so *that* was how they did a spin, but how did they manage to stay on their toes for so long? Such a vigorous and energetic dance this was—if only such a dance were danced at all those dull ceremonies he went to, then he might actually look forward to them. That thought was heretical, however, and he must never think it again. Suddenly there were four dancers again, then two. Ah, another cartwheel and a back-flip, and—cursed Nobleness' there was a late arrival blocking his view.

Obviously the only solution was to climb onto the boards under the railing, presumably put there to keep the smaller children from falling into the river. Flutirr did so, leaning forward once more. Ah, even better than before. He could see over everyone's head, instead of having to rely on the whims of the classless to lean far enough apart for him to see the dance. One of the dancers was moving to the other side of the fire; he would have to lean forward more to see. Standing on tiptoe felt precarious, but he could hold on with his arms. Now how did *do* that with those ribbons, and . . . *ouch,* one of his hands slipped on the railing. He hastily groped to get it back in place but the other hand slipped too. Suddenly he couldn't find the railing to hold on to anymore. His elbows and his knees were bumping and scraping against wood. His head hit something, then his back, and he found himself in the water.

He opened his eyes but they stung so he closed

them again, which only made them sting worse. He tried to spit out the water in his mouth, but that made more come in. At the same time he was trying to get to the surface, only he wasn't quite sure what direction was up and what was down. He thought he felt sand with the tip of a finger, but he wasn't sure, so he clumsily moved his limbs about. He found the sand again, but now that he had found the bottom he didn't know what to do with it because he was still worrying about the water in his mouth. He spit it out again, and again it didn't work and he swallowed some more. Then somewhere around his feet he seemed to feel something tugging at him, then there were hands everywhere pulling him up. Next, he was choking, but this time he seemed to be getting the water out and no more was coming in. He was moving somewhere, and finally he felt the ground under him. He coughed out the last of the water in his mouth and carefully peeled his eyes open.

On the opposite bank, there was no fire; he must have floated down the river. But that didn't make sense, for here was the bridge so close he could almost touch it—and then he saw his rescuers, and in the faint moonlight he was able to make out their clothes.

Flutirr, future President of the High Council of Trilene, and possibly a future representative on the Supreme Council of all Centre of Nelvins, had been rescued by Nelvins who were lower than the fleas on a rat and did not even exist.

The classless ones seemed to realize the significance of the situation in the same instant, for the ones who had dragged him ashore abruptly dumped him to the ground and leapt away, as though Flutirr's skin could poison them. Flutirr heard more than one colorful curse being hastily muffled by a hand. More loudly and clearly was the chopped question: "What the Nobleness is this Noble—" Flutirr made a weak attempt to pull his feet under him. How to get out of this situation? Should he simply leave? When he was still so weak he wasn't sure he could manage more than a undignified crawl?

"We can't leave him like this," came a harsh whisper from somewhere in the midst of the hovering classless ones.

"He is a Noble. What would he have done for any of us if it had been us drowning?"

"We could get killed just for touching him to drag him out of the river—how can we touch him again?"

"Whatever he may have done, Jeffie, whatever may happen, Beje, he is cold and wet, and needs the fire. Your Most Supreme Nobleness, are you able to walk?"

Flutirr violently jerked in shock. A classless one, daring to address him! He struggled to pull himself to his feet, but collapsed. The classless one who had addressed him pulled him up, and supported him. His unNoblish touch seemed to burn his skin. "Let's go to the fire, your Most Supreme Nobleness," he said. Flutirr only dug his fingers into the shoulders of the classless one to steady himself, then shoved the classless one away. Flutirr's own parents never touched him—how could he let filthy vermin do so? But Flutirr was not quite ready to stand on his own. He tottered for a moment on his feet and almost fell before two classless ones hastily lent their hands for support.

Flutirr partly walked and partly let himself be dragged to the fire where he crumpled to the ground. Someone draped a blanket around him, and when he examined it, he found it was made form a patchwork of tattered rags. Still, it was warm, and he drew it tighter around him. A Nelvin handed him a bowl of hot broth. Flutirr shoved it away, spilling broth everywhere. It was bad enough that he had allowed these vermin to help him to their fire and that he had sat there and accepted the loan of a blanket. To eat their food as well would be even worse.

"Looks like this one can't eat our food," the Nelvin with the broth said impassively, as he slowly drew a piece of cloth from his pocket and wiped the spilled broth from his hands. His face showed no reaction, but it was not the frozen face of a Noble. It was the face of a man with too much quiet determination ever to be wounded by an insult.

"Perhaps he's just not hungry. Come sit down, Ramie." The Nelvin frowned slightly but sat beside the woman who had spoken to him. All the Nelvins shifted uncomfortably.

"Come, let us keep on with the dance," another

Nelvin said. Two dancers stepped near the fire, and now Flutirr could see that the ribbons they wore were every bit as tattered and worn as the blanket he was using now. Then they began to dance, and once again the blur of colors captured his attention like a magic spell. He dragged his eyes away and stared into the fire. He mustn't let them think he actually enjoyed their primitive dance. He must proudly represent the whole of the Noble class. Still he couldn't help sneaking a few peeks at the dance and a few curious glances around the circle. He caught a few classless ones staring at him, then looking quickly away. Then he watched the exchange of dancers: four dancers, then two again. Then the two old dancers removed their ribbons and gave them to two new Nelvins. Now that he was watching up close, Flutirr realized that the dance never used the same two Nelvins twice. That meant each Nelvin probably danced no more than a few moments throughout the entire night.

Slowly Flutirr's shivers stopped, and somewhere at the back of his mind was the vague thought that he didn't really need the fire anymore, or the blanket. He should be giving up both so he could go home. Instead, he stayed, dozing off for a few moments, then watching the dance a while, then watching the fire, then watching the other Nelvins. He saw a few leaving to enter their huts, presumably to sleep. For a moment, he wished he had a hut here to sleep in too. There were also occasional Nelvins waking from their sleep to join the circle, so the number of Nelvins stayed fairly stable. Apparently no one stayed awake all night. The dance ended, and there was an awkward moment when everyone sneaked glances at the High Noble before the storyteller stood.

"There were a few lads who asked me to tell the tale of the two Nobles and their adventures. Because of circumstances y'all know about, I will save that tale for another time, and tell the tale of a beautiful Nelvin lass." Many of the Nelvins stole covert glances at Flutirr. Clearly the aborted tale was less than complimentary to Nobles. He pretended not to notice the glances and kept his gaze on the fire. "Now this lass dearly loved a lad who was the handsomest lad in all the village. She dearly wished to marry the lad, but the lass was a Low Tolerable, and the lad a High Tolerable. So it seemed there was nothing for her to do—"

The voice meandered through the tale. Flutirr tried to listen, but somehow the story couldn't hold his interest at much as Duucaniel's tale had. There were frequent pauses, as though the Nelvin couldn't remember the story, or was even inventing it as he spoke. Flutirr dozed fitfully, hearing the tale only in snatches. The girl did a good deed (Flutirr slept through the deed) and was promoted to Mid Tolerable class. Meanwhile, the High Tolerable fell in love with the "lass" and stole twenty Jublas from a Low Respectable in order to be demoted enough to marry her for a "delightful hundred 'leven years." Somehow Flutirr did not feel the same satisfaction at this happy ending that he had at the last tale. Even when he had managed to focus his attention for several consecutive moments, the story had still seemed disjointed, as though some of the scenes had been edited. Perhaps, he thought, they were offensive scenes edited because of his presence?

"Night, y'all," the storyteller called out as he hobbled away on his cane. There was a polite collective murmur. For a few moments, there was awkward silence, then someone spoke:

"I'd best be putting the kids between their blankets. Junie looks asleep already."

"Yeah, I'll be doing the same now."

These two simple sentences, like the first spark from two sticks that have been rubbed together, set off a flurry of chatter. The conversations started to blur together, so Flutirr gave up trying to listen to any of them. He catnapped, and when he woke only a few Nelvins were left. Probably his being here had made everyone leave earlier than usual, Flutirr surmised.

The first thing he heard was someone saying, "G'night, going to sleep now. See y'all in the morning."

"Sure thing, Kipper. Oh, and Kipper, you hear any more of your son?"

If anyone noticed Flutirr's sudden alertness, they ignored it. "No, nothing more."

"Hope everything's okay, Kipper."

"Thanks."

"Yeah, well, good luck. Sleep well."

"Same to you, Reffie . . . everyone." He nodded tersely and left.

"Hey, Don, isn't it time you got some sleep? It's only a little while till dawn. You'll really have to sleep a solid night tomorrow."

"Yeah, Dad, I *know*. I'm going. 'Night."

It was the same Nelvin Flutirr had seen at the bridge that long-ago dawn. So, he could speak after all, though he did have a slight lisp. Don stood—and hugged his father. Flutirr stared in astonished horror—why, that was one of the most unNoblish things anyone could do. Only very young Noble children ever received that kind of attention, and Don seemed to be about his own age. He should have outgrown hugs long before now. Flutirr sharply drew his gaze away and frowned into the fire, trying not to remember how long it had been since the last time he had been hugged, and trying not to hear the insistent voice in him that said: *It's not fair.*

'Y'know, Reffie, if I were a Noble hanging around here, I'd be thinking about getting home around this time."

"Yeah, I would be too, Beje."

"Wouldn't want to get in trouble, after all. Y'know, say somebody were to notice you've come from here, and don't believe the tale 'bout almost drowning."

Flutirr stubbornly kept his gaze on the dead cinders of the fire. These Nelvins were as rude as he'd known lower-class Nelvins were, giving such blatant hints that they did not appreciate his Noblish company. He might have stayed forever, just out of spite, but he

72

did have to leave eventually, He tossed his blanket on the ground and left.

"Well, going to bed now, then," Flutirr heard as he crossed the bridge.

Chapter 7

IT was a horrid piece of news obtained at great risk—he had kept expecting the Medicine Tester to halt any moment and ask just why he was asking such a queer set of questions. Tonight, if mad impulse hit him again, he would take the even bigger risk of relaying his news.

Flutirr nibbled on his wild nut pastry (he had been smart enough to come earlier this time) and made his way to the bridge. After finishing his snack, he sat on the bridge and slept until the music woke him. Flutirr rubbed his eyes in a clumsy, unNoblish manner and looked toward the fire. The music, he noted, was not quite the same as last night, but the dance was not very different.

Flutirr stood and walked to the center of the bridge, wisely avoiding the trick that had toppled him into the river the previous night. Still unable to see clearly, he walked a little farther. There, that was better. He stood admiring the twirling ribbons and intricate steps until his legs grew tired from standing. Reassuring himself that he could always see more the next night, he sat on the bridge and napped. When he woke, the stars told him it was little more than two hours until dawn, and the silence told him the dance was over. He started to stand until he heard the familiar voice of the storyteller. "Now that we have none of these pesky Nobles around here, I can get to the tale of the two Nobles I was about to tell last night.

"Now, there were two High Nobles named Lylurrre-Sill-Rrre, who I shall name by the name of Lying-Lyrics, and Hillliri-Tesi-Si, who I shall name Hillock." Flutirr smothered a sharp intake of breath, almost shouting a protest at this horrendous mutilation of the Noble names. Those were the names of the husband-and-wife Copresidents of the Supreme Council of all Centre of Nevins! It was scandalous for even a President of a High Council to refer to one of them by his or her calling name, let alone make such a disgusting mockery out of the name. The Most Supreme High Nobleness Rrre was certainly not a liar, and the Most Supreme High Nobleness Si was not at all comparable to a hill. Furthermore, the storyteller had also butchered the pronunciation of their names, pronouncing the noble sounds of *lll* and *rrr* as ordinary letters. Flutirr's hand unconsciously went to the hilt of his sword.

"Now, these Nobles were like every other Noble, lying if they felt like lying, bribing to get their way, and all other Noble things." There was a murmur of amusement from the circle, and Flutirr could feel his sixth finger twitching furiously. "So, these Nobles joined the Supreme Council of all Centre of Nelvins because both their families had been High Nobles for so long they were completely noble in every way, and because they were the oldest High Noble lines in all the land, they were President together.'' There seemed to be an almost steady stream of laughter, occasionally swelling and then softening again.

"Then one day a pair of strangers came to Trilene and said to Lying-Lyrics and Hillock that they wanted to duel with the pair to the death on the wager that whoever won would win the whole estate of the loser. Now, the noble pair weren't too keen on the conditions, but naturally it would not be a noble thing to say no!'' There was a brief pause as the storyteller let the laughter fade away. "So there seemed to be nothing to do but fight the duel. They did the noble thing, and chose their swords and chose their clothes with care, and they hired the best duel trainer in all the Centre of Nelvins. Then as the day of the duel dawned, they went to the chosen site—and with them were the two chosen Respectable fighters!'' There was a brief round of applause at this satiric description. "Now this pair of strangers saw the Respectables and said they wanted to fight only the noble pair and no one else. Lying-Lyrics and Hillock pleaded with all their might, but still the strangers said they would fight the noble pair and no one else.

"At last Lying-Lyrics and Hillock saw the strangers could not be convinced. They agreed to fight, but still they pleaded some more to have a full Lightingball cycle to study the art of dueling. Even a mere Bluelantern cycle would surely be enough to learn all they needed, or so they thought. But nay, said the strangers, a Dewlight cycle, twenty-three days, is all you need. They all went their ways, and the noble pair started to train that very day for half an hour every day. And since this was far more work than they had ever done before, they thought it would be all they would need!'' There was a wave of appreciative laughter. ''The day of the duel dawned once more. Lying-Lyrics and Hillock met the strangers at the site, and began to fight. Now at first, it seemed easy to the nobles to simply swing their swords back and forth, and forth and back, but they soon found the strangers were far better then they could ever be.

''On they fought, and soon the nobles were felled, and over them stood their enemies with swords swinging around and around over their heads, ready to strike! There was room for either noble to lunge his or her sword right to the strangers' hearts, but the nobles had never been so near to death in their lives, and froze with terror, like any other noble!'' There was more laughter. ''And so it seemed they would die. Then along came a twosome of classless Nelvins, and they were quick to see the danger. Swiftly they ran to the scene, grabbed the noble swords, and killed the strangers with a single blow each! The nobles stood to brush their clothes, and turned to thank their saviors. Then they saw the classless clothes and were ashamed to see they had failed where classless Nelvins had won. They took their swords from their saviors, and killed them with a thrust to hide their shame forever.''

Flutirr literally trembled with anger. It was slander, it was libel, and he *must* report it. He should be striding across the bridge right now, swinging his sword in his hand, and see what they would say then about his Noblish sword, and about the lack of courage he was supposed to have, and see if they laughed at him then. And that ending to the story, that ending was the worse of all—it wasn't true, it couldn't be true. Nobles were better than that; they would surely have recognized the bravery of the classless ones at least enough to allow them to live, and it didn't matter anyway, because if such a thing were to actually happen the Nobles could have handled the duel without any kind of help. The whole cursed story was a lie, a fluffing of their overgrown egos. They just wanted to imagine that they were braver than any Noble.

Flutirr scurried back across the bridge just before the classless Nelvins began to cross, glowing lanterns in hand. He sat at the foot of the bridge and cursed the story some more, and finally he found himself repeating a hypnotizing litany to himself over and over in his mind: It wasn't true, it wasn't true, it's all a lie, it's all a lie and it isn't true, isn't true, isn't true, all a lie, isn't true and all a lie and all lies and lies and lies and it isn't true, and it wouldn't happen like that, they're lying and lying, lying, lying, lying, lying.

The classless Nelvins crossed the river, quietly chattering about this and that and the story and the way it ended and don't you miss the flowers so sorely, and that was an amusing story, wasn't it, except the ending of course, and how're things going with you and oh, couldyaloanme bit 'f oil for my lamp? At the edge of Flutirr's mind was the vague thought that he ought to be furious with these disgusting, disrespectful unNoblish Nelvins. He ought to hate them and their unNoblish ways, their unNoblish dancing, their unNoblish chatter, and their unNoblish stories. He shouldn't be here at all, especially not for the reason he had returned that night. The soft voices rippled intimately through the darkness, and Flutirr closed his eyes, almost swaying with the soothing rhythm of their words.

Before long the multiple footsteps faded away. A few moments later, the first tremulous notes of a flute came. The flute murmured through the air, gently urging, giving some message, if only Flutirr could *(Come, come, whispers the breeze)* decipher it, it was so faint he couldn't quite get it *(come with the breeze)* and he really wanted to understand so desperately *(golden, glowing, tall reeds)* or if he just let himself go he would *(pianissimo melodies with the wind)* understand what the music was trying to say—*(birds fluttering, birds chirping)* that had sounded like a real bird, he would have to learn how to— *(bird play, bird chatter, pecking meals among the reeds)* and he had thought his flute was at home, he must have put it on his belt without knowing it, now how— *(wind bending the reeds, sharing tender indecipherable words with the wind, sun shimmering, birds scattering, sing-*

ing, wind pushing through the air, come away, come here and hear the birds sing like no other bird, come, peace, beauty, peace) and Flutirr blew one tentative note on his flute without even knowing he was doing so, and, abruptly, the music halted.

What had he done? That was such stupid thing to do—he should have had better control of himself. It was things like this that got you gray marks and loss of respect and, therefore, loss of power. But this line of thought was ludicrous, because what did power (important as it was) have to do with music, and getting Don to start playing again? He tentatively breathed a few notes from the beginning of the song *(Come, come, whispers the breeze).* It was not nearly as good as Don's version; the playing was too stiff, too precise. He would have to loosen up, playing *this* note slightly longer than the meter told him to, and the next slightly shorter. And *these* notes ought to flow together so it could sound more like a breeze— but then came the birds, and he did not know how to do those, so he hesitated.

Chirrruh, rrr aahhh, said the flute across the bridge. Flutirr waited, but there was nothing more. *Chirrruh, rrr aahhh,* he tried to say with his own flute, but it came out more like *Ch—i—r—ah, r ahhhuh? Chirrruh uh,* the other flute encouraged. *Ch—i—r-r-r—* Flutirr stuttered. Three simple notes floated across the bridge, and Flutirr repeated them. Then came the notes again with a rapid succession of three more notes that Flutirr recognized as eighth notes. Or even shorter notes, if that was possible. In fact, that blurred sound of the bird song must have been made of a series of numerous notes far shorter than eighth notes, Flutirr finally realized. He imitated the lesson, then attempted an experiment of his own, trying to create any sound that would remotely resemble a bird. What came from his flute, however, sounded more like flowing water. *Come, come, murmurs the brook,* he played experimentally, and for a moment his flute blended perfectly with the brook below. Startled, he stopped. He could make his flute sound like a brook!

More music trickled its way to him, and Flutirr knew that what he had achieved was nothing compared to what was possible in the hands of a master. This boy made the very stones sing, the very light on the waters tinkle, and the very grasses on the riverbank whisper poems of warmth. Flutirr's hand literally trembled with eagerness, and no longer did he curse the unNoblishness of the song. Someday, he vowed, he must play like that. Then for an instant, he felt of stab of irrational jealousy of this boy—if only he himself could have started to play music like this long ago, instead of being subjected to the constant regime of Noblishly defined songs, then perhaps Flutirr would be just as skillful as this classless Nelvin was now.

The brook faded away. Footsteps rang on the bridge. Flutirr leapt to his feet—he mustn't forget what he had come for. His movements must have made some noise, for Don jerked his head in Flutirr's direction and froze in place at the opposite end of the bridge. Don stared at him, awkwardly holding his shorter leg behind him ready to be dragged forward. Flutirr hesitated a moment at his side of the bridge then crossed, stopping right in front of Don. He then broke the most severe law in Nelvin society, nearly always punishable by demotion to classless status. To some, such a fate might as well mean death.

"Don," he said, stammering slightly, "Don, tell Kipper . . . his son will not be given the medicine until the later stages of the disease." For a moment, his lips parted, but he couldn't think of anything more to say so he turned away.

"Your—Supreme High Nobleness?"

Flutirr looked back.

"I will tell him."

Flutirr nodded once, tersely, and continued his way up the path.

Chapter 8

A street looms in front of him. A long white street that seems to be stone one moment, and oddly pale dirt the next. He steps forward, and sees his right foot step on the road then disappear when his left foot swings forward. And so he walks. Then to either side of the road there are houses, then there are Nelvins. The Nelvins jostle about in a swirl of colors. He is the only one in the middle of the street; all others stay on the sides. After a minute, he notes there is no noise, then, just as he notices that, the noise comes of a thousand voices chattering, a thousand voices arguing, a thousand voices bartering for the best bargain.

Barter? Then this must be the market tables downtown. And now, he does indeed see these tables on either side of the road. But why, he wonders, does no one see me? And why, he wonders, do I walk in the middle of the road? Why do I—a Noble—walk in the middle of the road?

Everyone turns to look at him, pointing, jeering.

The faces leer, the eyes seem to grow in size.

Classless, classless one, they seem to say.

A pair of huge, starving black eyes stare into his own—whether they are cursing him, or pleading for some unnamed desire, he cannot say.

He wants to flee, but suddenly he cannot. Each step is an awkward struggle as he tugs his clumsy shorter leg forward. (When did that occur? A moment ago it was fine. But does it matter how it occurred, when the important thing is getting out of here, out of eyesight?) Then comes the longer leg, moving to the side, swinging in a circle. Forward and forward. The road must end.

The road does not end. But it must, his mind protests.

It does not.

His hands tremble with fear. Must he go on and on, among these faces, among these pointed fingers? What if they were to begin to—

The first stone comes, then more, in a shower of sharp pain. Finally it ends, and it is dark. He opens his eyes, and still it is dark. There is only a soft shimmer of moonlight from his window.

Window? Where is he now?

His hands cautiously poke about. Soft, something soft. Like a bed. He pulls his feet from under the covers and places them on the floor, then sits on the side of his bed, shivering.

* * *

Light, light, he needs light.

He needs to walk about, to shake away the monsters of the night.

Flutirr silently, swiftly, dresses in the dark, and leaves.

Downtown, did he really need to go downtown? It ought to be enough just to walk a few blocks, then return to sleep the rest of the night away.

Yes, yes, he needed to go downtown.

He walked down the road, only it was real now, and not a dream. The red-tinted lights eerily lit the way until he was beyond them. Then there was the sky full of stars, like the sun of day shattered into a million shards, then flung into the black air and trapped there. The moons dangled among the shards, like three clusters of shiny juminkin nutshells, collected, and clumped together into the shape of one near sphere, and two crescents. Then, at last, there was the brook, and there was the fire. Flutirr stumbled on the bank, and only then did he realize the swiftness of his pace; at times it had been almost a jog as he had rushed to the brook. He vaguely thought, What an unNoblish thing to do. Then he wondered, Did anyone see me? But he brushed the question aside as irrelevant; he was here, and that was the only important thing.

Flutirr stood, and brushed the dirt off his clothes. They felt damp now—the grass and soil by the brook were wet from the water. He knew his clothes were probably grass-stained and muddy, but it did not matter, since they weren't his best clothes anyway. He went to the center of the bridge, but that wasn't enough to chase away the nightmares of the dark. He crossed the bridge and sat at the foot of it on the other side. There, that was better. It put him closer to the fire, so he could almost feel its warmth. Hypnotized by the swirling ribbons, he watched the dancing until it ended to make way for the storyteller.

The storyteller that night told several short, amusing tales instead of the long suspenseful epics that were his usual fare. The night wore on, and at the end of each tale, the circle grew smaller. After a time, only two Nelvins remained to linger near the fire. They seemed to be lovers, for they sat side by side murmuring words Flutirr could not hear, and touched each other on occasion. They parted when the first Nelvins left their huts with lanterns. The workers headed toward the bridge, startling Flutirr into scurrying for cover. As the footsteps reverberated overhead, Flutirr cursed the inattention that had trapped him on the wrong side of the bridge. Now he would have to wait and hope he would not be discovered.

After a fraction of an hour, the whole area seemed abandoned. Flutirr planted his feet on the ground, crouching under the bridge, debating a few seconds with his body about whether it would be capable of running across the bridge swiftly enough for him to escape discovery. Then it was too late, because there was Don coming toward his usual spot under the bridge. Flutirr fidgeted a little more, still on his haunches, not certain that he wanted Don to find him here on his own territory. He almost sat, finding his current position awkward. Then he decided that it wouldn't do for a classless Nelvin to be able to literally look down upon him. What was the use of four feet and eleven inches of height if he never took advantage of it? He stood, brushed off his clothes, and directed a scornful glare down his nose, looking right into Don's eyes when he approached.

Don didn't seem to see Flutirr until he was only a few paces away from him. Flutirr was able to detect the precise instant he did so, for Don froze in place and stared at him. A mix of emotions swept through his Nelvin-black eyes—astonishment, certainly, but the other reactions were indecipherable. Flutirr would have almost sworn that anger and resentment were among them. Then Don closed his eyes for a bare second too long to be described as even a slow blink, and his gaze became properly humble. There was nothing in Don's stance that hinted at disrespectfulness, but Flutirr's High Noble–trained eye for body language detected tension in his every muscle.

In an attempt to sound as casual as if he appeared there every day, and spoke with classless Nelvins on a regular basis, Flutirr said: "Don, you did give the news to Kipper?"

"I did . . . your Supreme High Nobleness," Don responded.

"Did he take it well?" Flutirr asked.

Don did not answer instantly, seeming to be discomfited by the question. "I am afraid not at all well, your Nobleness. But he had not truly expected otherwise.''

There was an awkward silence, and Flutirr almost left. Somehow, though, he could not make himself respond so brusquely after discussing such a delicate topic. "You may offer him my condolences, Don," he said.

Don nodded stiffly. "I will, your Nobleness."

The conversation seemed to have come to a logical end, but still Flutirr lingered. For lack of anything else to say, he said: "So—you beg every day?"

There was a flicker of surprise in the other's eyes, then annoyance and caution. "Yes, your Supreme Nobleness, from dawn to sunset, and sometimes beyond."

"I do not suppose you get much, do you? How do you manage to get enough to feed yourself this way?"

"My family always shares, your Nobleness. As long as someone has had a good day, that makes up for those who have had a bad day."

"But you do not all beg, do you? I have heard some of you work."

"That is so, your Supreme Nobleness."

"But if you do not exist, what would make anyone dare hire you?"

"We work under Low Tolerables, your Nobleness, or Mid Tolerables. We are hired by messengers in the city, or nut pickers at the nut plantations. They get paid by the amount of work they do in a day. If they hire one of us to do the work with them, then twice the amount of work gets done, so they get paid twice as much, your Nobleness. That is how they get the money to pay us, and that is why they hire us."

"And the Low Tolerable merchants—they take money from classless ones when you want to buy food?"

"No, your Nobleness, for they always think we have stolen the money. We get paid in food and cloth, your Nobleness. The money we often throw away, for it is useless."

"The way you play the flute, Don, you must get much food."

"Some, your Nobleness. And money."

His reply was delivered in a manner most Nobles would have described as rude and impudent. He spoke too bluntly and directly, most Nobles would have believed, to suit one of such a lowly station. The rudeness was subtle, but it was there. Flutirr would have to keep an eye on this Nelvin.

"But I have seen you only with the flute. Do you not ever play other instruments?"

"I have tried, your Nobleness. I also play the harp, accordion, violin, and piccolo. But Nelvins like my flute the best, so I play only that. It brings in the most food."

Even in Nelvin society, where everyone dabbled with every instrument at least once, and studied at least two in depth, five instruments was still an astounding number to master.

"Then you must know more instruments than any other Nelvin in your—in your settlement," Flutirr said.

"Yes and no, your Nobleness. Those who have jobs all day play only one instrument, but there are a few others who beg all day also. The beggars of the town, your Nobleness, always study at least three instruments."

"How is that these Nelvins who work do not make the effort to study more than one instrument?" Flutirr asked scornfully.

"You have seen them leaving the town, going to the city, before it is dawn."

"Yes."

"Many do not return until long after dark."

Don had made his point, but Flutirr was too irritated to admit that a classless Nelvin could be right and a High Noble wrong. "If they are so busy all day, how can they find the time to watch the dancing and listen to the stories each night? Why do they not use that same time to practice their second instrument?"

"Because at the nighttime sessions they perform on their *first* instruments, and it is impossible to play two instruments at the same time."

If Flutirr was bothered by the classless Nelvin's rudeness, he was not shocked into speechlessness for long. "I have heard only two or three instruments play at a time," he refuted.

"But not by the same players all night, your Nobleness! You cannot expect any ordinary Nelvin to work himself to a dragon-heat all day, then come home to play music until his fingers bleed into nothingness! We all take turns, except for the beggars who

92

play all day. Were you not able to recognize the different styles of each Nelvin?''

"No, I was not," Flutirr said reluctantly, and with an edge.

"Well, of course you Nobles are not taught to play with individual styles. Naturally, it would be difficult for you to recognize the shifts in players when they occur, your Nobleness.'' Flutirr could not determine if Don was trying to make amends by excusing his ignorance, or being scornful.

"Perhaps."

Don said: "If you would please excuse me, your Nobleness, I normally use this time to practice the flute.''

In a fluid, Noblish motion, Flutirr gestured beside him. "Of course. You are permitted to sit." He used the form of "you" that, in Nelvinese, meant: You are nothing. You are not even dust, for dust, at least, exists. You do not.

"Since I typically sit where you are standing, it would be much appreciated if you would kindly move. Your Nobleness.'' The pause before Don's last two words made the title of respect seem an insult.

"Perhaps this is where I want to sit this morning?''

"Does it matter where either of us sits, your Nobleness?''

"Perhaps my education has been flawed, but it seems to me that it ought to be common courtesy to give guests first choice in seating arrangement. Even classless gakkha like you ought to know that." *Gakkha* was Nelvinese for unsterile or poisoned earth. In an economy that was dependent on good soil for nut trees, in a society that was once made almost exclusively of farmers who lived and breathed the land, gakkha was the most despicable substance imaginable.

"Wh—gak—why, you—*you're* the one who destroyed whatever hope Kipper had left, then you even gave him *condolences,* for Nobleness's sake, as though that'd make everything better, and you screw up my songs at dawn with your Noble trash, then you expect me to welcome you, to worship you—don't *you* interrupt me, just because you're dressed in blue and purple and boots expensive enough to clothe and feed the whole town for a year! And *you* think you're *noble,* for Nobleness's sake, when all of you are nothing but sneaking, conniving, manipula—"

And Don went pale. Flutirr felt the sixth finger of his left hand twitching furiously as he stepped forward. He tightly clutched his sword in the air. Briefly, Don's body twitched all over, as though he were about to run, but then he stood still once again. He looked almost comical as he tried to stand straight on one short leg and one long leg, and tried to look brave with a mouth as asymmetrical as his legs. Flutirr moved his sword back, ready to swing, seeming to contemplate just how and where he would strike.

Chapter 9

T HE two stood in the predawn darkness, observing each other in the moonlight. The nearly-full moon hung directly over Flutirr's shoulder at that moment, glinting off his sword.

Flutirr's arms began to tremble. His sword dipped in the way a sword moves at the beginning of a swing—

Flutirr lowered his sword and hesitantly sheathed it in the scabbard at his waist. For a moment, he seemed to hover on the edge of speaking, but there was nothing that he could say to one he had been about to kill. The silence went on, for neither were there any words Don could say to a Nelvin who had just decided to let him live, but who still had the power to change his mind.

Flutirr finally saw there was only one thing for him to do.

He released the hilt, which he had been holding the whole time the pair had been silent. He raised his hands to his neck and unfastened his cape. He was tempted to swing it about him in a dramatic, Noblish gesture, but he restrained himself, and only removed it, folded it, and put it on the ground before him. He unbuckled his scabbard with its sword, and kneeled to put this, too, on the ground, diagonally across his cape. He stood and waited, though he knew not what for.

Don, no longer pretending to be either humble or brave, studied Flutirr's face in silence. At last, he said: "Dawn is nearly here. We ought to begin."

Flutirr stared at the suddenly equanimious Don. Then, for the first time, he began to see more than the small, scrawny, crippled body that Don inhabited. He saw, instead, the stubborn strength in Don's steady gaze that had given him the courage to confront a High Noble. And he also saw the—*nobleness* that permitted Don to set his enmity, however temporarily, aside. In that moment, Flutirr thought briefly of stepping away from where he stood to allow Don to seat himself at the spot they had argued over. It would be Flutirr's way of acknowledging the Noblishness of this classless one. Then suddenly a flash of rage swept through him. How could he permit himself to admire, to even *like,* a classless one? No, he would not move from his spot.

Nevertheless, Flutirr felt an inexplicable stab of guilt when Don sat where Flutirr had indicated he should sit at the beginning of their confrontation.

"I usually like to begin with a few of the Lìntrill scales," Don said, and the two began to play. The

Lintrill scales was a collection of scales created centuries earlier by the Respectable Jevi-Quew-Lintrill for nearly every instrument in existence. Everyone in Nelvin society knew most of these scales by the age of five, so Flutirr had no difficulty playing along with Don. When they stopped, Don spoke again, with his lisp coming through heavily: "What would you like to play this morning?"

Flutirr hesitated, then commented: "The last time I tried to imitate a bird, it sounded more like a brook. You could show me how you do a bird."

"Um—I think to begin with, you—" And then he had trouble with the next word, for it appeared that all Nelvinese synonyms had too many r's for him to handle with his lisp. Then Flutirr deciphered the odd sounds Don was trying to create.

"I need?"

"Yes . . . to learn to do a trill, like this," and Don showed him a trill. When that was done, Don showed him some other things that sounded a little like a bird, but not quite. Just when Flutirr was about to ask what any of these things had to do with the sound of a bird, Don said: "If you would put these together—what is your name?"

"Sinie-Tilll," he said, giving his secondary and primary family names.

"What is your name?" Don said again, more firmly. Flutirr stiffened—Don clearly wanted Flutirr's calling name. Even a Mid Noble would not have dared take such a blunt approach.

"My name is Flutirr."

Don nodded in acknowledgment. "Flutirr. Now if you would put these notes together—" Then he played a bird song on his flute, the kind of song one hears in the early morning saying a sad farewell to the stars, and mournfully speaking of the sunrise that too must die as soon as it is born. Flutirr awkwardly attempted the song, but Don interrupted him continually. His every note, it seemed, was criticized. He needed to think of the piece as a whole; he needed to concentrate on a particular passage that was giving him trouble. He needed to let the notes flow; he needed to keep the notes from turning into mush. He needed to play naturally; he needed to play in a new manner until it felt comfortable to him. When Flutirr made a few irritated comments, Don halted his criticism to ponder.

"Flutirr, what do you think of when you play? What picture do you have in mind when you do this piece?"

"Picture? What do pictures have to do with music?"

Don looked incredulously at Flutirr. "Why, they have everything to do with music! You have to have some idea of what the composer meant by a piece to keep it coherent when you play it. You need a picture, a conception to shape your playing—a picture that changes and grows as you change and grow, yet gives steady guidance to your music. Don't you *ever* do that when you play?"

"Nobles do not play that way," Flutirr said stiffly.

"Oh. Of course you don't. You can't show your emotions. Nevertheless, to learn a bird song, or the sound of a brook, you need to learn not just the notes, but also how to play those notes with feelings. They need to sound a little like a bird, and a little like your soul."

"But how can you reduce a soul into a logical mathematical equation that could work as a song?"

"Mathematical equations? For music?"

"That is the way music is done."

"Among Nobles, perhaps, but not among us. How can you appreciate our music if you think music is akin to math and numbers? If it is not the feelings in our music, then what is it you like about our music so much you want to learn it?"

Even a Noble would have had difficulty guessing what Flutirr was thinking behind his frozen face. "You say I am supposed to be thinking of pictures while I play?" he said neutrally.

"Yes. You need to create, to think of—wait. Let me say it a better way.

"Flutirr, the first time I saw you was the day I played a song about the sun. Did you understand it?"

"Yes."

"How did you know it was about the sun?"

Flutirr made some vague, not very Noblish, gesture. "That is what it sounded like to me."

"*Why* did it sound like the sun? What was it about the way I played that made it sound like the sun?"

"The music was assertive and firm, yet light-footed like the rays of the sun," Flutirr said, feeling foolish. His words were so unNoblish they sounded almost poetic.

"Yes. And what else?"

Flutirr felt even more awkward. "The music . . . I know this makes no sense, but it was warm and sweet, the way you would expect the sun to smell if it had a smell—I know that's stupid because you only hear music, not feel it or smell it—"

"No, no, that's good, it's good. That's exactly what I was trying to get across in my music. When I played that piece, I held a picture in my mind of a bright, happy sun that warms the grass, making it smell sweet. Then I tried to make my music match the picture. I knew what notes I had to play, so I didn't need to think about what they were—I concentrated on my picture of the sun, so I could make others feel the sun on their faces and smell the grass, not just hear the notes.

"That's why I keep telling you to think of the piece as a whole, Flutirr. It's not enough to move your fingers on the holes and try to make every note sound like it came from a bird. You have to pretend to *be* that bird, Flutirr. You *are* a bird, you have feelings you want to make others feel, and your only language is music. Play, Flutirr, and this time don't be Flutirr—be a bird with the soul of Flutirr with something to say."

Flutirr shifted uncomfortably, not accustomed to

being exposed to such passionate words that lay one's heart so bare. And he was made more discomfited by the answering echo within him, the hidden part of him that had always chafed at the Instructors at his school who expected him to do no more than move his fingers on the holes of his flute in the proper, Noblish manner. This classless one was like him—he, too, thought music ought to go beyond a superficial blend of mere sounds to *communicate* something—

Flutirr tore himself away from his unNoblish thoughts and brought his flute to his lips—but then he did not know how to play. Don was expecting him to say something with his music, but he did not know what one could say with nothing but air and a stick of metal. Then he saw the marvelous colors of the sun flicking its first rays against a few lazy clouds. What would a bird think of that, he wondered briefly, then tried to play what he thought a bird would say in response. He began to imitate the song Don had taught him, but it did not quite fit what he wanted to say, so he added a trill where there ought to have been no trill, and played a series of ascending and descending notes where there ought to have been a trill. *What doth this wonder do here?* he tried to have his flute say. *More beautiful than the day before, this wonder be!* he made his flute exclaim. *Why, these colors be even brighter than mine very own plume!* And some-how, his flute seemed to say those words almost as though it had acquired a vocal chord.

"Yes, you have it now! That's just what I meant!"

"But it is not quite the way you did it—I changed some of it."

"Flutirr, I never meant for you to imitate me precisely. I only intended to give you a few basic melodies that you could use to practice on, to get a feel for how to play. This time, you added more feelings to your music. I could hear your bird, and I could hear your bird's awe. There were parts I did not understand, but that isn't meant as criticism. We can't always understand exactly what another Nelvin is trying to say with his music. Part of the joy of music is trying to understand what the composer and player are saying with their music. Do you understand?"

"I think so."

"Good. It's about time to go."

"Yes. I need to get home myself."

They stood, and Flutirr donned his class symbols once more.

When they were ready to go, Flutirr stood aside and let Don pass before following. Nelvin custom required the lower classes to walk in front of their superiors—a custom originating from the theory that inferiors must be closely watched at all times lest they commit some evil act. The pair walked down the path, one after the other, until Flutirr turned to see the sunrise.

"Don, I would like to hear that song you played of the sun."

"There is not much time, Flutirr."

"Just the first part."

They stood a brief time as Don played.

"That—was very nice," Flutirr said.

"Thank you, Flutirr."

"I wish I could play like that," he whispered into the morning chill.

Chapter 10

FIRST, it was guilt that kept him from returning. On one hand, he loved the music Don had taught him, the beautiful sparkling music he had longed for so long to play. On the other hand, once the light of day and the ordinary routine of school with his fellow High Nobles returned him to his senses, he began to regret his rash behavior. How could he have conceded so much on that night—his sword, his cape? He had, at least, kept his dragon-leather boots on, despite Don's remark about how they could've fed the whole town. He had also retained his Noblish shoulder-to-waist sash. Still, all he had meant to do was convince Don that he wasn't going to kill him. No need to take off the cape too. That was like saying that Don was as good as Flutirr!

After the guilt receded a little, he had a cluster of exams in one week. He simply didn't have time to spend gallumping about downtown, much less with classless Nelvins. Even, Flutirr had to tell himself firmly on more than one occasion, one who played music like that, and who seemed as if he would be an interesting sort to get to know. It was, accordingly, two weeks before he made his way back to that fire on the other side of that bridge over that river out in the country.

He listened to the music that night for the transition of players Don had told him about, and this time he heard it. He listened, also, for the distinctions between each musician's style of playing, and now the differences were glaringly obvious. How had he missed these qualities before?

The last of the ribbons trailed through the air, and the last of the songs was played. The storyteller stood and told an adventure tale about, of all things, an infant dragon who spoke. It required much more suspension of disbelief than Flutirr was accustomed to, but he wound up enjoying the bizarre tale. When the circle began to disperse, and the fire was left to die, he started keeping an eye out for Don. A steady stream of Nelvins beat upon the bridge over his head as he waited. After a few moments of this, a Nelvin flashed his lantern under the bridge. "Your Most Supreme High Nobleness," he called. Flutirr, hidden from the lantern in the shadows, froze. What in Nobleness could be going on? How had this classless Nelvin known he would be there? Why would he wish to speak with him? Why would Don have told this Nelvin of Flutirr's presence?

"Your Most Supreme Nobleness, if you would honor me with your Noblish presence?" Flutirr did not move. The Nelvin crossed the bridge, then was gone. Flutirr waited until the last of the classless Nelvins crossed. He waited until the sky became purple, then gray. He waited until, at last, he saw that Don was not coming this morning. He stood, and brushed off his clothes, then massaged the muscles that had become stiff and cramped. More than ready for breakfast, he left.

When he returned the next night, Flutirr pondered how he should react when he saw Don that night. Should he question him about why he hadn't been there the previous night? Or should he wait and see if Don brought it up himself? Best to flow with the rhythm, he decided.

Just like the other night, a Nelvin split off from the rest, and flashed his lantern under the bridge. "Your Most Supreme High Nobleness, if you are present? Your Supreme Nobleness?" The classless one paused a brief moment before turning to cross the bridge. Flutirr did not stop him.

And, again, Don did not come that morning.

The next night, Flutirr went to wait for the mysterious lantern-carrying Nelvin. The Nelvin came at the usual time, calling in the usual manner. "Your Most Supreme High Nobleness, I would wish to rest eyes on you?"

Flutirr came from the shadows and stood beside the bridge. "You are permitted to speak," he said.

"Your Most Noblishly Supremely Highest of all High Nobleness," the Nelvin stammered. "Your—

your—would you wish me to kneel, your Most Supreme Nobleness?''

The Nelvin did not know the proper way to act with a Noble, Flutirr scornfully observed. One never asked if a Noble desired one to kneel. One simply knelt whenever in doubt and left it to the Noble to grant him permission to stand again. For a very strong moment, Flutirr was tempted to say, Yes, do kneel, do kowtow, do grovel to me. Then the temptation went away, and he felt a twinge of guilt, as though it was wrong to want a classless Nelvin to show respect.

"That will not be necessary," Flutirr said. "You may speak." And when he spoke his last command, he used the Nelvinese "you" that is used to address those only a little below oneself.

"Your Most Supreme High Nobleness, I bring you a message from Don."

"From Don?" Flutirr exclaimed, then hastily attempted to hide his eagerness. "Yes, speak of it."

"Your Nobleness, I must inform you that Don will not be playing his music here anymore. He is now very ill, your Most Supreme High Nobleness."

Ill. That was a word Flutirr had always associated with colds and flus. Yes, he himself had almost died of an illness, but he had been an infant then. He did not even remember what illness it had been. No one he knew had ever become really ill, except for a remote cousin of somebody his mother knew, who had died of some bizarre disease a few years ago. Don could not really be all that ill. "He will, of course, be cured eventually," he said, partly as statement, partly as question.

"That is doubtful, your Highest Nobleness. He has Sporadasm."

Flutirr wanted to say something, but could think of nothing. He tried to speak, but his mouth would not move in the right way.

"Don sent me to tell you, your Supreme High Nobleness. He is not in the delirious stages yet; the dizziness and fevers began just a week ago. Is there something you would wish to say to him, your Supreme Nobleness?"

For one more moment, his tongue was paralyzed, then at last it was free. "Could I see him?"

The Nelvin hesitated. "I suppose if you stand in the doorway, it ought to be all right. Just be careful, your Most Supreme Nobleness. Sporadasm is contagious."

Flutirr was led to a worn gray hut indistinguishable from all the rest. Flutirr opened the door but saw nothing besides two piles of rags on the far side of the shanty. The classless Nelvin beside him called out: "His Most Supreme Nobleness is here to see Don."

"Is he then? Don, sit up, you have a visitor." One pile of rags was suddenly transformed into an elderly female Nelvin who scuttled to the other pile of rags to help Don raise his head.

"Oh, Flutirr, that you there?" Don said, his words barely coming through the lisp that seemed heavier than it had ever been before.

In a screechy, scolding voice, the elderly Nelvin admonished him: "Don, this is a High Noble, you must address him properly. Your Most Phenomenally Noblishly Supreme High Nobleness, please, please don't see fit to slay him for his rudeness to you, your Supremely Highest—"

"Enough! This is not necessary," Flutirr snapped.

"Of course. You've already given me your Most Noblish permission to live," Don said. Flutirr did not miss the sarcasm of Don's words. "So, Flutirr, come to see me in my last days?"

Now Flutirr felt foolish. What point was there in seeing Don at a time like this? He was going to die. He could no longer play music in his state. Flutirr had nothing in common with Don, other than the music they played together. "I wondered why you never appeared the last two times I was here," he said coolly, Noblishly.

"Well, now you know."

"Has the past week gone w—" Flutirr let the last word trail into a mumble. Don was dying; how *could* his week have gone well?

"Other than coming down with Sporadasm, your Nobleness, my week has been most marvelous, your Nobleness. My Noblish mansion, your Nobleness, did not cave in on my head, your Nobleness, nor did any one of my servants disobey me this week, your Nobleness. Would you like to hear more, Flutirr?"

Flutirr stiffened his jaw to keep from flinching. He had already been exposed to some of Don's anger, but only now did he realize that cold hatred went behind it. "That won't be necessary," he said.

"Then you are not here on a social visit? Did you, perhaps, expect me to play more of the flute for you?"

"Of course not."

"Then, if I have your Noblish permission to ask, why are you here?"

Flutirr said nothing for a moment, trying to formulate a response. That was the advantage of being a Noble among inferiors; you could stand forever saying nothing, and no one would interrupt your thoughts.

The inferior, however, did not oblige him.

"Well? Have you no answer?"

Desperate for words that would not reveal how clumsy he felt, he spoke flippantly and arrogantly. "There is always something that can be done about every disease. I thought I might as well see what I could do."

Don made a noise of disbelief, and it was the classless Nelvin who had led Flutirr to the hut who responded to him. "Your Supreme Nobleness, I am afraid that there is nothing, unless you were to search for those in the west, beyond the Centre of Nelvins, who are said to know more than we—even the cure of Sporadasm. They are called the Hijj."

A cure for Sporadasm? Flutirr trembled with hope. Perhaps there was a chance that Don—

He pulled his thoughts from their unNoblish path just in time, and sent them in a more proper—and more realistic—direction. When he spoke, his voice was once again arrogant.

"If there is truly such knowledge, why have the Nobles never heard of it?"

"Your Nobleness—any Noble, or even a Respectable, would kill us if we even approached one. We could not have told you of these Hijj even if we had tried."

Flutirr winced. The classless one was right. If classless Nelvins were the only source of such valuable information, there simply would be no way for anyone else to discover this knowledge. How many Nelvins, Flutirr wondered—classless and ones of class alike—had died all the time the Nelvins of class had refused to pay heed to the classless?

How many, for that matter, had died while these classless Nelvins had apparently done nothing to find the cure even for themselves? It was true that the life of a classless one was not as valuable as the life of even a Tolerable. Nevertheless, what was one supposed to think of Nelvins who evidently did not care enough about the lives of their own children and families to make the attempt to defend themselves against such a dreaded illness? "Why do you not send messengers to find these Hijj, and obtain this knowledge for yourself?" he said.

"That would be impossible, your Most Supreme Nobleness. We have no horses to travel with, your Nobleness, and the journey would be too long on foot. We earn barely enough food in a week just to feed ourselves during that time without saving more for a journey, your Nobleness. If we were injured on the way, no one would help a classless Nelvin, your Most Supreme Nobleness. Even those who are not Nelvins hesitate to help us, and will not always let us earn our food or lodging, your Nobleness. Besides, everyone is sorely needed to support those who can't support themselves, your High Nobleness. There is no one here to make such a journey.''

''Then I will make the journey,'' Flutirr said scornfully, without thinking twice. Wherever he had to travel, it could not be nearly as difficult as the Nelvin made it sound. What was impossible for a classless Nelvin shouldn't be so difficult for a Noble with Flutirr's level of education and wealth. And everyone would surely be willing to help a Noble. The task ought to be easy for him.

''Your Supreme Nobleness, are you sure you desire to do so?'' the classless one said.

''Of course I am. Where do I find these creatures who know so much?''

''Your Supreme Nobleness, I am afraid we know only that they are west of here, and that they are called the Hijj. We cannot tell you anything more precise than that.''

''And I am supposed to believe these creatures actually exist, and would actually help cure Don—when you cannot even tell me anything about them?'' Flutirr's initial rush of hope began to wear off, and wariness set in. How much of what this classless one said could possibly be true?

''We are aware, of course, that stories can be exaggerated, your Nobleness. But there is enough consistency in the tales for us to believe that the Hijj can truly cure Don.''

"All right then, I will go look for these Hijj. How far must I travel?''

"All the tales, your Nobleness, say that the Hijj are about a Bluelantern's cycle from here, even on horseback.''

At last confronted with the enormity of the task before him, Flutirr was silent. A little more than forty days each way was a ten-week round trip. It could easily take almost as long as a Thunderball cycle. He would be missing an extraordinary amount of school at a time when he could least afford to do so. It was not that he liked school, of course, but he didn't dare to fall even further behind than he was, and risk additional marks. He would also have to come up with a convincing excuse for his absence or the Nobleness knew what his parents would do.

All this traveling, all this inconvenience, would be based on a big gamble that the Hijj even existed, let alone actually knew anything. Even if they did, there was the risk that the Hijj would not give him the cure. Even if luck stayed with him to this point, he had no reassurance Don would even be alive when he returned with the cure. It did take a long time to die from Sporadasm, but it didn't take forever. Considering the enormous effort it would take, and considering the low probability of success, it was clearly ridiculous even to think of trying. Don was, after all, only a classless Nelvin. There was no reason to be so upset over the prospect of a classless one's death that he should go tramping across the land of Trillilani chasing classless tales. Perhaps this was really for the best; it allowed him to make his break with these classless ones quickly and cleanly, with few temptations left to draw him back to the river.

"I will go," he heard himself say.

Chapter 11

THE classless Nelvin looked at Flutirr in astonishment. "You will, your Supreme Nobleness? But—but then, you will need a horse, we must find you a horse, your Highest Nobleness. And you will need food and money. How soon can you leave, your Most Supreme Nobleness?"

"It will take time to find a plausible reason for my parents to allow me to make such a long journey, and then, as you said, I will need food and other things. I have a horse of my own already, I need only to get her from the stable."

"Your Supreme Nobleness, your parents would not, I presume, approve of the real reason for this journey?"

"No, they would not."

"Then perhaps you oughtn't tell them. It might be best, your Nobleness, if you didn't talk to them at all. Do not even use your own horse, your Nobleness, or everyone will know you voluntarily went on this journey without informing your parents. You must leave tonight, your Supreme Nobleness. Even a single day could make the difference for Don."

Flutirr was flabbergasted. How could this classless Nelvin presume to tell a Noble what he should do? "Tonight? But what of all the things I—"

"Or at the very least, first thing in the morning when you can hire a horse, your Supreme Nobleness. You do, I hope, have money with you, your Most Supreme Nobleness?"

"Perhaps I do," Flutirr said stiffly. A Noble, of course, never discussed such matters with the lower classes.

"Your Most Supreme High Nobleness, I did not mean to pry, but I must know if I am to help you plan your journey. Do you have sufficient money to hire a horse, your Supreme Nobleness?"

For a moment, Flutirr was tempted to lie, to say that he had no more than one or two Jublas. Then he would go home, and make all the arrangements for the journey himself, thus regaining control. But then he panicked. Where would he begin? What supplies would he need? Was the classless one right when he said that Flutirr should say nothing to his parents, or should he make up an excuse in advance? And if so, what excuse could he use? There were too many factors for him to even think about. So he did not lie. "I believe I have sufficient money for a horse," he said cautiously.

"Good. And if that runs out later, you can always earn your way by playing your flute, your Nobleness. I may be able to find a little food to give you, though you won't need it until you enter the wilderness, your Nobleness. Come, let us see what I can find for you in my hut.''

"But what of my parents? And the Instructors at school? How would I explain a sudden absence like this?"

The Nelvin paused. "Perhaps—perhaps you can say you were kidnapped by a band of Humans for one of their bizarre religions. Would that be all right?"

"That is the most ridiculous idea I've ever—"

"Flutirr," Don said, "the only other plausible excuse is to tell everyone you are going to save the life of a classless Nelvin. Would you like to do that, Flutirr?"

"Of course not," Flutirr muttered.

The classless Nelvin waved his lantern about. "Now then, we'll need paper to write a note on, and a water bottle for you. Several of my children are messengers, your Nobleness, so there ought to be some scraps of paper around somewhere. I'll be off to my hut, your Nobleness, if you'd stay here."

"Yes, certainly," Flutirr said faintly, not enthusiastic about setting off on a long journey without the chance to get a full night's sleep first. Why, he scolded himself, hadn't he been firmer with the classless one?

"So, you really are going?" Don said.

"Yes."

"Well, I wish you the best of luck. You will need it."

"Thank you," Flutirr said clumsily, before he realized how ridiculous it was for him to be thanking

Don. He was doing this journey to save Don's life; Don should be thanking Flutirr, not the other way around.

"Let's hope you succeed."

"Yes, I do hope I—" Flutirr stopped. To complete the sentence would mean entering a part of him that was too tender for him to even think about.

"Why do you do this?" Don said.

"It just seemed a waste to . . . to let your disease take its course while doing nothing," Flutirr said, then he chafed because he couldn't decide if his words had been sufficiently vague.

Don studied him thoughtfully for a moment. When he spoke, Flutirr could not tell if he was being serious, or if he was making another attempt at needling him. "Is it, perhaps, because you view me as a friend?"

"Nobles do not make friends with—" Flutirr's tongue stumbled over the words, because he was suddenly uncertain whether he really wanted to say what he was going to say. "I am not your friend," he said instead.

Again, Don studied him. "You are not wholly like other High Nobles," he said. It was clear that Don had meant his statement to be a compliment, so Flutirr started to thank him. Then he realized that most Nobles would not take this as a compliment, so he did not.

The classless Nelvin returned with the supplies for the journey. The moment Flutirr had finished taking inventory, he said, "I will be going, then."

"See you on your return, Flutirr."

"I'll—" Flutirr started to say, then the full impact of Don's words hit him. See you on your return, Don had said. How can you, Flutirr wanted to ask, if you may be dead? How can *I* see *you*, if you may be dead?

Don't die, he almost said—then, horrified, he spun away. He could not let Don see that the Noblishly tight skin of his face had begun to twitch, and his Noblishly calm hands had begun to quake. Walk, he told his legs—and tremulously, his legs took him away from Don and the other classless ones.

In his head beat the litany: *Don't die. Please don't die.*

Chapter 12

FLUTIRR stifled an exasperated sigh. There was simply no path into this unNoblish forest. Once again, he prodded the mare he rode into trotting along the edge of the woods. He was almost tempted to turn back, to halt the whole journey that had brought him here—but he could not. Whether his parents had received the forged note or not, and whether they had believed the forged note or not, the consequences would be the same for Flutirr if he returned in ten days or a hundred. Besides, Flutirr certainly could not give up after traveling a whole week from the Centre of Nelvins to the Secondary Centre of Nelvins to the forest.

It had been an easy week, though disorienting; he had never been outside Trilene in his life. He had been tempted to linger in L'han, in K'yumi, in Pinjune, in the Secondary Centre of Nelvins, so he could do some sightseeing. Everything had been, however, disappointingly the same as Trilene. Besides, he could not distract himself from his assigned task. So he was now at the edge of this forest—surely there *had* to be a path. How could the residents of the Secondary Centre of Nelvins not clear one for travelers like himself?

Evidently the local Nelvins had indeed been negligent of this task; all Flutirr's hunting failed to uncover anything remotely resembling a path through the dense trees and tightly woven bushes that lay before him. Flutirr bit back a curse as he dismounted his mare. He had been astride for nearly half the morning, which only compounded the aches and stiffness he already had from a week of heavy riding. Any major motions, such as dismounting a horse, aggravated his aches even further. He walked in circles, leading his steed after him, in a futile attempt to work the cramps out of his muscles. Facing the inevitable, he mounted his horse again and directed her into the forest.

Well—this was not so bad. It was slow going but not an unpleasant ride. Flutirr had been told that it might take him as long as a week or more to work his way through the woods. He could understand such a generous estimate now; there seemed to be no end in sight to these massive, densely grown trees, and he had to pick his way through the undergrowth with caution. He was not enthusiastic about living away from the physical amenities he was used to—but, still, he was not overly concerned about being in the wilderness itself. He saw nothing, so far, that was in the least threatening. Except for the continuing soreness of his muscles, it seemed he would make his way through the woods in perfect comfor—

A tree branch abruptly disagreed with him by slapping him in the face, nearly scratching his eye. Flutirr irritably shoved the branch away, getting his arms scraped in the process. If this kept up, Flutirr thought to himself, his forest ride would cease to be a pleasurable experience. Indeed, here was a second branch that insisted on shoving itself into his face. He grabbed the newly offending extension before it could knock him off his mare, and carefully ducked under it.

A week in the woods—that meant a week of dodging these infernally unNoblish branches, and otherwise fending for himself. Flutirr may have found reason to dislike the prospect, but at least he still had no need to fear for his safety. He was, after all, a High Noble. It was precisely here that his Noble's training, upbringing, and education should give him an edge in survival. At the age of twenty-three, Flutirr had gone through over seventeen years of schooling—that had to count for something. Somewhere in his extensive education, for instance, he must have learned what to do when the sun was beginning to disappear, and it was nearing time to sleep, with no inn in sight.

All he could think of was Duucaniel, of the classless storyteller's tale, sleeping in the bushes.

No, no. There *had* to have been something he had learned in school—but Flutirr could think of nothing.

Very well, then. He would dismount, feed himself, then sleep in the bushes. The classless tales may have deviated more than once from real-life detail, but what other logical solution was there to Flutirr's problem of finding a place to sleep? Flutirr hoisted himself to the ground and began rummaging through his food packs for his first meal in the wilderness. But wait—in all the adventure tales the storyteller had told, the travelers had always built a fire before eating. And to build a fire, he would need to find some firewood before it became too dark to look.

Flutirr left his steed and plowed his way through the forest, hastily surveying the forest floor for any substance that looked like it might burn. He returned an hour later in near-complete darkness with his arms full, and dumped his heavy burden to the ground in relief. He prepared to start a fire—only to suddenly discover that he didn't have the least idea how to do it. The servants at his home always used flint, but he had no stones with him. How had the adventurers of those tales done it? Flutirr racked his brain, but could remember only the phrase "the weary traveler built a fire." Then he remembered: the storyteller had once told a brief, amusing tale about two bumbling Nelvins trying to set a fire. They had succeeded, at last, by rubbing two sticks together. Could that work in real life?

Flutirr gave it a try. And another try. And a third. Only then did he remember that the pair of Nelvins in the tale had originally failed because they had used firewood soaked by rain. Every piece of wood Flutirr was using was damp from being dug up from a bed of heavy moss. Nobleness, Flutirr cursed. Surely he didn't need a fire to eat anyway. He stood and blindly flung away the pieces that were in his hand. Perhaps the next night he would—

A sudden, terrified neighing came through the darkness, then the sound of a panicked gallop over uneven forest-ground. Confused, Flutirr looked about him in time to catch a glimpse of a raised tail vanishing among the trees. His mare seemed to have escaped, which was impossible because he had tied her securely to a nearby tree. The very moment he had dismounted, he had—

He had rummaged through his food pack, then gone looking for firewood. He had completely forgotten to tie his mare—and just now, he must have accidentally hit her with the firewood, startling her into a gallop.

That meant he had to chase his mare through the trees and the dark, or he would be stranded without food and water. Of more long-term concern was the threat of having to walk all the way to the home of the elusive Hijj on his own two feet. Flutirr took off after the mare, calling out: "C'mere, you! C'mon, whoa!" After an undignified half hour of stumbling his way among the trees, Flutirr found the mare quietly waiting for him, grazing on some unidentifiable plant. When she saw him, she serenely snuffled through her nose, just as though she hadn't forced Flutirr into unNoblish exertions just a few moments before.

"Oh, *you* look content," Flutirr said. He was so worn out he didn't have the strength even to try to return to where he and the mare had been before. His steed had brought all the needed supplies with her, and Flutirr had his flute and his money bag at his belt. Nothing had been left behind, except a pile of useless firewood. Flutirr tied his mare to some bushes, ate, and awkwardly crawled into some nearby bushes. Just like Duucaniel, he reminded himself. If Duucaniel could do it, then a High Noble like Flutirr could too. All he had to do was imagine himself on a Noblish adventure, bravely enduring the prickly bushes—*ouch*.

Ah, yes. And the unNoblish biting bugs too.

Flutirr did sleep that night, but in the morning, he felt more itchy and sleepy than he did heroic—and an empty, grumbling stomach was surely not definitive of heroism either. The latter, at least, was easily remediable. He sleepily groped for the supply bags he had left on the ground the night before.

What he found brought him wide awake with horror. His bags were not neatly propped against a nearby tree as he had left them, but lay haphazardly on the ground several feet away. Half their contents seemed to be scattered about, as though they had been ransacked the previous night. From the tiny footprints on the ground, he guessed that small animals had done the task. Flutirr pounced on the bags to survey the damage. Just as he had feared, much of his food was now gone. There was still enough for three or four days, but he would have to ration himself carefully. He would also have to learn to build a fire to scare the animals away at night, and find a better way of protecting his supplies. He could not afford to lose any more of his food.

A subdued Flutirr pulled his things together, ate a few bites, and moved on. The next few days were uneventful ones. He suffered more hours of dodging branches and struggling through undergrowth. An increasing hunger nagged at his stomach, but Flutirr sternly reined in his hands when he found them drifting—as though they possessed minds of their own—to one of his supply bags. Each night, he worked himself into a sweat struggling with his firewood. The first two nights, it took him from an hour before sunset until complete darkness before even the first sparks of his fire appeared. The task of building a fire became increasingly easier with time—nevertheless, it chafed at Flutirr. He was a High Noble, doing a servant's job—a job without skill, yet he was continually fumbling it. Flutirr endured the humiliation; he had to do it to survive.

One day, Flutirr discovered a bush full of berries. Eager to fill his empty stomach, he gobbled down half a dozen handfuls of the ripe, juicy fruit before slowing his pace. He stored some of the berries in one of his supply bags. They were almost as good as wild nut pastries! Flutirr remounted his mare, and tried to clean his sticky mouth with his purple-stained hands. He was feeling so full he was sure he could wait until as late as the next day before eating again. It might be two days before he ran out of berries and had to dip into his dwindling food supplies once again. Flutirr contentedly pressed his heels into his mare's sides.

Everything was proceeding as he had originally expected it would; minor discomforts existed, but all his problems were eventually solving themselves.

By that evening, Flutirr was sure he was dying. There was no other answer, he thought as he leaned into the bushes for the tenth time that day to vomit the nonexistent contents of his stomach. He had to be dying. Why else would he feel so feverishly hot? Why else would his stomach be heaving so often, and twitching so constantly in between? Why else would Flutirr feel so weak he could not even sit properly? He had been such an unNoblish idiot to eat those berries. Why hadn't his school taught about such things?

But, of course, school was not for learning about practical survival skills. School was for learning Noblish music, and for learning to read, write, and calculate. School was for learning to be a proper High Noble—or a proper member of whatever class you belonged to. Nobles, especially, would not be taught about the mundane details of day-to-day life—most of them would always have servants to care for such things.

Flutirr now rode with his head resting on the neck of his steed, and occasionally shivered with flashes of chill. He knew he should halt his journey and sleep in the bushes, but something kept him moving. Perhaps it was the vague hope that someone would discover him, out here in the midst of nowhere, and help him. Or perhaps he was spurred on by the thought of

Don's fragile figure lying in his dark ramshackle hut, struggling against death.

As soon as Flutirr began even to consider the latter explanation, he pushed the thought away. He did not actually care about Don himself—he was simply doing the journey as an act of extreme generosity, Flutirr told himself. He, a High Noble, could not let himself care about cla—

A spasm passed through Flutirr's body, and he was unable to complete his thought. He rode onward until dusk, and forced himself to build a fire before going to sleep. For a long time, however, he could only shiver as he lay on the ground, and gaze vacantly at the odd sight of leaves and stars hovering above him. His sleepy eyes still expected to find the familiar images of his High Noble ancestors looking down upon him from his bedroom ceiling. Could he truly be dying, Flutirr wondered. Was this what it was like to face death—the pain, the chills, and the shock of looking upon a strange leaf-and-sky ceiling in the final confused moments before one's dreams?

By the next morning, the vomiting had passed, and Flutirr found that he stood on his feet more steadily than the day before. He had not, after all, been dying. When he mounted his mare to begin a new day of traveling, he yanked a few leaves from the nearest tree and pressed them to his face: he was *alive!*

Chapter 13

Oɴ the tenth day in the forest, Flutirr saw an opening in the trees. As he came nearer, the opening turned into a field. He was almost out of the forest when he realized he was on a farm—and *there*, in the middle of everything, was a cottage. It was not a mansion, like those Flutirr was accustomed to seeing in his home district. Nor was it a multifamily complex like those in other districts of Trilene, or a ramshackle hut like those in the classless settlement. But it was, at last, civilization! There would be Nelvin voices. Perhaps even Nelvin music. And above all, a roof, and no more bugs! Flutirr almost ruined some of the plants in his eagerness to reach the cottage.

The door to the cottage opened, so Flutirr reined in his mare (he had finally managed to master the technique). "Hello th—" he called, then he caught a glimpse of the Nelvin's hair. It was a burnt red—which made no sense, for no adult Nelvin had anything other than black hair. She turned, and now Flutirr could see she was not a Nelvin, but an Elvin.

This was utterly horrible. How in the land of Trillilani would they communicate in Flutirr's less-than-fluent Elvinese? What if the Elvin didn't even speak the common Elvin dialect he had been taught?

The Elvin became aware of him, so he was forced to stammer his way through a few Elvinese sentences to communicate his desires. In the end, he had to suffer the unNoblish indignity of using hand gestures to get the Elvin to understand him. That done, Flutirr pulled a few Jublas out of his money bag so they could negotiate the cost of his lodging. The Elvin nodded her head up and down in the universal gesture of negation.

"Nelvin money," she said in infantilized Elvinese, pointing to the multicolored bills in Flutirr's hand. "I, Elvin," she said, gesturing to herself. "Crowd houses, Elvin," she said as she gestured westward. So there was a town—a crowding of houses—nearby. He would have to stop there to get more food. But in the meantime, how could the two of them agree on payment if this Elvin didn't even accept Nelvin money?

The Elvin made an incomprehensible gesture, and called out something that sounded like a name. A male Elvin, evidently her husband, came from the next room, and a rapid discussion was held in Elvinese. The male turned to Flutirr and gestured that he be followed. Flutirr was led outside to a pile of wood. In a few coarse, unNoblish gestures, Flutirr got the message: he, a Noble, was expected to do the menial job—a *Low Tolerable*'s job—of cutting wood. This, apparently, was these Elvins' idea of fair payment.

Flutirr thrust his money in the Elvin's face, and argued and fussed in a bizarre mesh of Nelvinese and Elvinese in his attempt to get him to take money, not work, as payment. Nothing worked. Flutirr resigned himself. This would, at least, be better than suffering another night of bugs.

He was to chop the wood the following day, the Elvin indicated. They went into the cottage as the last shreds of light seeped from the sky.

Dinner that night was the oddest concoction Flutirr had ever eaten. The only familiar item on his plate was the garden vegetables. There were no sauces on any item on his plate, nor was there a nut anywhere in sight. The bread was served on the side, instead of under a sauce. There was nothing but a discolored lump of something the Elvins called *cheese* to go on the bread. For the main course, there was a rectangular piece of pastry stuffed with what seemed to be some kind of pale meat mixed with a mysterious substance the Elvins described as a grain similar to rice— whatever rice was—and another substance that looked like boiled leaves.

Flutirr had gone without sauces while in the wilderness, and, of course, had to forego bread as well, not having anything to balance its dry, floury texture with. Nevertheless, this meal was wholly different from even the diet he had followed in the woods.

Who, after all, had ever heard of meat (if it was meat) as a *main course*, rather than appetizer? And, furthermore, how was he to eat with this strange flat eating utensil with the blunt cutting edge, instead of the normal spoon he used every day at home? Flutirr almost made some excuse not to eat at all.

The bread, in fact, turned out to be far better than any he had eaten at home, and the cheese made it even better. The meat was tender and juicy, not the dried and smoked variety he had come to expect from the various meats imported into Nelvin territory. The leaves were a little salty and squishy, but flavorful. The meal, as a whole, was quite enjoyable, even with the distracting chatter of the Elvin couple and children. They all spoke, it seemed, upon whim. None of them ever tapped his or her water glass or wine goblet before speaking—they just spoke. A rather irritating habit, Flutirr thought.

But wouldn't it be terrific, Flutirr thought, if his own family did the same?

The windows of the cottage were closed up with pieces of some transparent substance—glass perhaps—that rattled in the wind at night. At home, such a sound would have kept Flutirr awake all night, but he had heard louder sounds in the wild, so he was able to ignore it.

Breakfast was as strange as dinner had been. The drink was cow's milk, not water, wine, or the milk of macoon nuts. The eggs were scrambled then fried—though at least it was done with good, fiery-hot spices—instead of poached and served sparingly as delicacies at dinner. There were even slimy strings of green called seaweed mixed with the eggs—though they actually tasted good. And they also tasted vaguely like the leaves he had eaten in the pastry the previous night; perhaps that had been seaweed too. And, again, bread was served on the side, and there were no nuts or sauces in the meal.

After breakfast, Flutirr was led to the woodpile, and left there to work. He found the axe impossibly heavy, and the pieces of wood equally bulky and difficult to move into place. In less than an hour, Flutirr was sweating, his hands were sore, and he had only a few pieces of cut wood to his credit. The male Elvin came by to check on his progress, and looked disapprovingly at him before correcting his stance, demonstrating the proper way to cut wood.

"Thank you," Flutirr said stiffly, feeling very foolish. Nobles should not have to be taught to do the simple job of a servant. He worked the rest of the morning, which was more than twice as long as he had expected to work. He thought he was finished by lunchtime, but then he found that he was also expected to bring the wood to a pile by the fireplace. That took another half hour, with the help of some of the children. Then, blisters and all, he sat to eat. More meat-and-seaweed pastry was served for lunch, this time with some of the spices he was accustomed to eating at home.

After he dropped his fork for the third time that meal (it hurt his sore palms to grasp anything), the

Elvin wife insisted on seeing his hands. An un-Noblishly tender look of concern crossed her face, and she gestured that Flutirr wait for her to return. She came back with ointment, and reached for his hands. Flutirr began to draw away, but it was too late: she had already grasped his hands, and begun massaging the cream into his blisters. Flutirr's hands flinched under her ministrations, but the twitches were not solely from pain. It was bad enough to endure the touch of someone from an inferior class—the touch of an inferior species was even worse. Back home, even the Noble Medical Specialists would have avoided physical contact by putting the ointment on a piece of cloth, and using a stick to spread it on his skin. That wasn't nearly as soothing as this Elvin's soft hands, but it was more Noblish.

After lunch, Flutirr was given extra bandages for his hands, and was pointed in the direction of the town. He cautiously picked his way through the field, then brought his mare to a steady trot the instant they hit a decent horse trail. It was evening by the time he arrived in town and located an inn. When he found the inn owner, Flutirr started to speak in Elvinese, but to his relief, the Elvin innkeeper knew Flutirr's language.

"Many Nelvin travelers come here," the innkeeper explained, "and some of them stay to live in the area—so, naturally, I had to learn your language, your honorness. So, how long will you stay?"

"Just for tonight, including supper," Flutirr replied. "How much is your lodging?"

"Our lodging for the regular rooms is forty Kits and thirty-four Kuts a night, including free breakfast and an evening drink. The Suite, which is free tonight, your honorness, is fifty-five Kits and thirty-four Kuts a night, and includes a drawn bath. Which would you prefer, your honorness?"

"I will pay in Jublas. Prepare the Suite."

"I'm sorry, your honorness, but we can't accept Jublas here. If you have no Kits, then I suggest you pawn something, like, perhaps, your cape. I do permit lodgers to entertain guests for meals—I presume you play that flute well—but I do not permit more than that."

"I will play my flute for your guests, but I will not pawn my cape."

"Then I am afraid you will find it difficult, if not impossible, to get lodging in this town."

Without saying a further word, Flutirr stormed out of the inn. What right did he have to treat Flutirr, a Noble—a *High* Noble—with such rudeness? What right did that innkeeper have to turn down his perfectly good money as though he were a scruffy-looking Low Tolerable dressed in rags who could not be trusted? And not only that, how *dare* the Elvin suggest he pawn something as valuable, as Noblish, as his cape? Even a Low Noble would never go anywhere without a cape. If that was the way he felt, Flutirr would take his business elsewhere.

Flutirr froze in place when he became conscious of his unNoblishly hurried pace. Perhaps doing so cleared his head, for it was only then that he realized how foolishly he had reacted. Both the Elvin farmers and the Elvin innkeeper had turned down his Jublas, so it was highly unlikely any other Elvin would accept them—and he still needed to load up on supplies. It was getting dark, which meant Flutirr also needed a place to stay quickly. This town was not the woods; he could not simply lie on the ground and curl up to sleep. Furthermore, it was not as though he had to sacrifice wearing a cape altogether; he could simply trade his current cape for both Kits and a cheaper cape.

Flutirr was already near the market area of the town, so finding a cloth-and-clothes stand was a simple matter. With a cape no fancier than one a Low Noble would wear, a few supplies, and just enough Kits in his purse to cover a night's lodging, he headed back to the inn. To his relief, the innkeeper didn't comment on Flutirr's short-tempered behavior.

"Normally, your honorness, I ask for a couple of hours of music in exchange for dinner, but since you Nelvins are supposed to be so good at music, I'll settle for an hour. Do you play anything other than the flute?"

"I play the harp. But the flute is what I brought."

"Ah, I see. Well, the dining hall is here. I'll announce you first, then you come up to the stage, okay?"

Flutirr looked where the innkeeper had gestured. The so-called stage was no more than a bare piece of floor, free of the wooden tables and chairs that crowded the rest of the room.

When Flutirr was called to the stage he had to fight an unNoblish urge to wipe the sweat from his hands. He had never given a performance before; he had previously played only to practice his music, or so his skills could be graded for school. Nervously, he plunged into the song he had been practicing for school before he had started his journey: "Ternary," by some twenty-second- or twenty-third-century High Noble. It was a heinously difficult piece to play, adapted, Flutirr had heard, from a simple piece intended for three flutes.

He began his piece in a room of near silence, but before long, discontented murmurs rose from the crowd. What could be wrong? He was playing quite well, with very few errors that Elvins would hear. The song was an intriguing piece that teased and invited the mind to follow its patterns. He did not like Noble music as much as he used to, but there were still some pieces he liked, and this one of them. So why didn't his audience like it?

When he was finished, the innkeeper appeared by his side. "Your honorness, don't you know anything better than that? My customers are starting to leave because of your music!"

"I have just played one of the most Noblish songs in—"

"Noblish?" The innkeeper exploded with a few Elvin words that Flutirr suspected were curses. "I should have known you were a Noble. Look, you've got to play something better than that, or I'll lose more money than I gain. No more Noble stuff, okay?''

"I will try," Flutirr said.

No Noblish music. That meant he had to try the music he had learned from Don. He closed his eyes so he could concentrate better and began to play. In a house of tobacco stains and gnarled wood, a clean river suddenly flowed. In an inn of curses and threats, a sweet bird sang. In a room scented with alcohol and questionable smells, a whiff of flowers and warm stones wafted through the air. Between crowded tables of loneliness drifted murmurs of friends and places where you could never be alone. It was only when he was finished that Flutirr realized not a sound had been made while he played.

"You play another hour like that, you'll get free lodging too," the innkeeper said. Flutirr almost jumped, since he hadn't seen the Elvin approach him. Then the innkeeper spoke gently, sympathetically: "If I may ask your honorness, when did you leave home?''

"Two weeks ago.''

"And how long will you be gone?''

"A Thunderball cycle or more.''

"Ah, no wonder you sounded so homesick. But, do, do play more.''

Flutirr tried not to let his distress show. How could he have let his feelings come through so clearly? How could he have let himself be so unNoblish, so *vulnerable?* And now he was expected to play more of the same kind of music.

Flutirr improvised a song about how he felt, about feeling vulnerable, about feeling guilty for feeling vulnerable, and about how much he wanted to express himself, even if it meant being vulnerable. He didn't like this song as much as the last one, but his audience seemed to disagree with him. He played some more, about rivers and mountains and being homesick yet at the same time being glad to be away from home and on the road. It seemed like only moments until the innkeeper, with clear reluctance, waved him from the stage so he could eat a well-earned supper. He was offered ten percent of the customers' tips if he continued playing, but he turned it down so he could get to sleep.

After all, he had another long day of travel before him.

Chapter 14

As the sun began to breathe a wisp of gray and pink light into the sky, Flutirr mounted his horse in front of an inn far from home and headed even farther away.

He asked someone, on his way out of town, if she had heard of the Hijj, and if so, how far away they were. To his surprise, she had indeed heard of such creatures, and they were little more than a Dewlight away. He asked himself, as he entered the wild again, how a classless Nelvin and an Elvin more than two weeks' hard journey from each other had each heard of the Hijj, but he, a highly educated Noble, had not. His previous ignorance could be partially accounted for simply because no school would be so irresponsible to teach about creatures that might not even exist, much less possess the great stores of knowledge attributed to them. But still, there were other sources of information—word of mouth, rumor, and private musings shared in the anonymity of dark night.

And there was his answer. A Noble's rumors consisted of which bill was going to be heard by the High Council, and which would not be heard, and what was going to happen to all the bills that got heard. A Noble's private musings were about whether this bill or that bill ought to be passed, and why or why not. Nobles did not waste valuable thoughts on stories that seemed to be half fiction. High Nobles were not able to share such stories without worrying about losing respect or power. Only the classless had reason or freedom to dream of creatures that could cure all your problems as miraculously as the classless ones seemed to believe the Hijj could. The High Nobles on the Councils, secure in their mansions, pampered by their servants, and given everything they ever desired, would never listen to such tales, so no one would ever tell them.

Flutirr set his musings aside and rode onward, through forests, over rivers, through meadows. The sun rose, and the sun set. Light smeared into dark, and dark withered into light. Flutirr heard bird songs he had never heard before, and tried to capture them all on his flute. At first, his mare protested at this odd practice by squealing and often refusing to move at all. The pair soon reached a compromise: the mare learned to endure (and later, even enjoy) Flutirr's flute, and Flutirr adjusted his music to complement his mare's own natural rhythm. They evolved a language between them of subtle muscle twitches that Flutirr used to guide his steed left, or right, or straight ahead, leaving his hands free to play.

And so the hours were spent, as rider and steed

journeyed through wood, by water, through fields. Flutirr discovered a host of small creatures that he struggled to put into music. If only he had a Nature Book with him! Hedgehogs, mice, and rats he was able to identify, for they lived in Trilene as well. Wild boar he thought he remembered from pictures. The rest, however, were infuriating mysteries whose names hung just out of reach.

It was during one of those moments when he was turning his memory inside out to identify a gray, bushy-tailed animal he had just seen, that, in the midst of green bushes, right underneath a wondrous interplay of sunlight and shadows, he saw the unicorn.

More accurately, it was the mare who detected it first, for it was only her abrupt halt that made Flutirr look about and discover the unicorn watching him.

For a long moment or more, Nelvin and unicorn remained as still as the mist that blurs the sun at dawn. This was not, Flutirr observed, an ordinary unicorn. Typically, he had been told, unicorn hides were as golden as sun-bleached fields of wheat, as smooth as sand polished by an ancient sea, with a gleam as healthy as Dewlight at her fullest. The Nature Books at his school had paintings of unicorns with hides of woven flower petals from the whitest of flowers, and manes spun from clouds, and tails made from clusters of stars and comets and the flaming meteorites that burned paths across the night sky.

The unicorn that stood before Flutirr was an exotic blend of blue and white, like a deep sea with frothing white crests at each wave. Its golden eyes looked serenely into his own, and its horn sparkled like a million juminkin nutshells. If only Flutirr could remember the name of its species—there were Golden Unicorns, Pearly Whites, Midnight Unicorns, Star Unicorns, Midnight Horns—in order of rarity. Then came the one before him, but he couldn't recall—

"Painted Unicorn," he said in relief, having finally remembered.

The unicorn briefly lifted its head and gazed at Flutirr with more intensity than before. It lowered its head as though making a bow, turned about as fluidly as water, and faded into the woods again.

Flutirr and his mare remained rooted to their spot a moment, feeling it would be somehow disrespectful to leave too abruptly.

A few days later, he stumbled upon a road that connected with a collection of tiny villages, so he was able to sleep under a roof for several successive nights. He earned the money for his living expenses by playing music for food and lodging where he was permitted to do so, and by pawning things when he wasn't. In one Dwaline village his hosts took his worn clothes while he slept, and replaced them with a brand-new suit by morning. For this, plus food and lodging, they asked as payment a single song. The cut of the Dwaline clothes was foreign, and the colors were all wrong. The Dwalines, however, seemed so anxious to please him that Flutirr didn't have the heart to reject the gift.

There was a town of Kuu as well. The family Flutirr stayed with generously polished and restored his dragon-leather boots. They had an annoying habit, however, of playing practical jokes on him, so he was happy to leave. There was a village of Elvins, and even one of Nelvins. Flutirr found to his surprise that the latter village imitated Elvin more than Nelvin customs, in food and even language. It made perfect sense when he stopped to think about it. The two nearest high-population areas were the Elvin village he had just left almost two weeks ago and another large Elvin village three days' travel to the north. It was only natural that local Nelvins had more in common with the nearby Elvins than with the citizens of the distant Centre and Secondary Centre of Nelvins.

Flutirr almost didn't stop at the village of Humans, but changed his mind upon hearing that it was almost the last village until the main road came to an end. Why forego one more night of sleeping in comfort, he reasoned to himself, just because he had heard a few, probably untrue, rumors about Humans?

It was, he judged later, the worst decision he had made to date, except for the poisonous berries he had eaten near the beginning of his journey. Every tale he had heard of Humans turned out to be true. Humans were cold, prejudiced, and arrogant. He had to knock on at least three or four doors before a single Human would consider taking him in for the night, and even then, the price that was asked was so exorbitant he couldn't afford it. In all, he tried perhaps fifteen or twenty houses before finding a household that, firstly, did not slam the door in his face and, secondly, was patient enough to try to cross the language barrier and discover what he wanted and, thirdly, was willing to put him up, and, finally, did not ask a ridiculously high price, and, additionally, was willing to reduce the cost in exchange for a few songs and labor.

One of the daughters in the family he stayed with considered herself a great scholar in the language and culture of Nelvins, yet she barely seemed to comprehend two words in three that Flutirr uttered. Even worse, she seemed entirely unfamiliar with the three main forms of address, much less their numerous variations. She continually addressed him as a common Nelvin would address his or her equals in class, and looked at him bewilderedly when he used the form of "you" that one would use to address one vastly inferior—as Humans were to Nelvins.

The Human girl also had some confused beliefs about Nelvin culture. She had somehow gotten the notion that he was a wandering storyteller who used his flute only to complement his tales. When he insisted the contrary, she went into a sulk that lasted the rest of the meal. After supper, he played a few flute songs. He even attempted a little improvisation on a fiddle one of the boys owned. He almost didn't because he was tired and irritated after an hour's effort just finding a place to sleep, but the boy looked at him with such a pleading look when he asked that he had to give in. It seemed, Flutirr observed to himself, that he was beginning to develop the soft spot that every Nelvin, even High Nobles, had for children. It was a sympathy that crossed class lines—

prejudice was too strong for Nobles to bring themselves to look twice at Tolerable children in all but the most extreme life-and-death cases, but it was not an entirely unusual sight to see a Mid Noble bending to bring some crying Low Respectable child to his feet after a fall.

He left the Human village the next morning in utter relief. At last, he could get away from the incessant questioning about him, about Nelvins, about his travels. He did not mind answering questions, it was simply very irritating to be asked those questions in the form only common Nelvins used to address each other, and annoying to muddle his way through the Humans' awkward language to get at the meaning, only to find they were asking questions such as: Do all you Nelvins dress like that? Do all you Nelvins eat like that, with just the spoon, and haven't you seen a knife before? Do you Nelvins really sleep with your musical instruments, I heard that somewhere, are you positive you don't? And is it true that you Nelvins have this . . . what, a law, a custom or something that you can't——until a year after you're married?

The girl had translated the last concept into a word Flutirr thought she intended to mean "kiss," but she blushed so much Flutirr suspected the actual term was some analog of "intercourse." It seemed the Humans' frigidity concerning sexual matters was more than mere rumor.

There had also been that brief, confused lecture the girl had given him about the origins of Humans that convinced Flutirr the Humans were suffering from some bizarre form of insanity.

"I must tell you that old tale about how Humans got to Trillilani," the girl had said. "It's a true story, you know. Maybe you can even use it the next time you tell stories. This story says that once upon a time, Humans lived way up in the sky on a star. They didn't even know about Trillilani—they called their star Earth. But they didn't want to live on Earth, they wanted to live on Trillilani. So they caught a silver cloud—actually, the stories say they used a silver bird, but that just has to be baloney, because there certainly aren't any birds, much less silver ones, that are big enough to carry Humans! So, anyway, they caught a silver cloud, and rode it all the way to Trillilani. They were the first Humans to come to Trillilani, and all Humans are here because of them. Isn't that just the most fascinating story you ever heard?"

Heavens? Baloney? Living on a tiny prick of light in the sky? Riding silver birds and clouds? Clearly these Humans were insane to believe such tales.

At each village, whether on the main road or beyond it, Flutirr would ask how far he had to go before he reached the Hijj. No two estimates seemed to jibe perfectly, and a few towns had no knowledge of the Hijj at all. One or two informants even insisted he was headed in the wrong direction. Almost everywhere, there seemed to be individuals who had heard of the Hijj—but nowhere did there seem to be anyone who could tell him their precise location, or even confirm that the Hijj actually existed. With each passing day, Flutirr's anxiety increased. It was true that most estimates of his distance from the Hijj followed a logical trend downward, and an overwhelming majority of those who had heard of the Hijj believed they still lay to the west. Nevertheless, the inconsistency of the data concerned Flutirr. What assurance did he have that he was not chasing a race of rumor-created ghosts? How much farther should he travel before declaring the Hijj to be nonexistent, and not worth pursuing any further?

Flutirr arrived at yet another Elvin village. He reached into his money bag to count his remaining Kuts and Kits, and frowned at the amount. Even assuming he could earn his evening meal with his flute, he still did not have enough money to cover a night's lodging. There certainly weren't enough Kuts to replenish his dwindling food supplies. Once again, he would have to pawn something. But what? The last time he had pawned his clothes, it had taken both his shirt and his pants and even his undertights and shoulder-to-waist sash to bring him enough cash to buy new clothing and other necessities. The clothes he now wore were one step above the rags of classless ones. He certainly could not pawn those. It would be foolish to sacrifice the speed of his journey by selling his horse—she was rented anyway, and not his to sell—and almost as foolish to give up his sole source of steady revenue by pawning his flute.

That left the trappings of his High Noble class: his boots, sword, and cape. Flutirr wavered. Selling his sword would give him more than enough cash to get a decent secondhand sword as well as a good week's lodging. It would, however, be impossible to get that new sword where he was; nowadays, only Nelvins seemed to make these weapons for their Nobles to wear. He would have to continue his journey without this all-powerful symbol of his authoritative position as a High Noble, which was unthinkable. If he sold the boots, he would have enough cash not merely for that night's lodging but for anything he could possibly need or desire for the entire remainder of his journey—and a long time afterward. It would, however, mean giving up an irreplaceable family heirloom.

The only thing left to pawn, then, was his cape. He could not hope to receive enough money for his cape to be able to replace this valuable piece of cloth with even the cheapest replacement, and still have money for lodging and supplies. But at least it would be better than being without a sword or a pair of boots. Flutirr walked down the street and found a merchant. It was over quickly: within moments, Flutirr was capeless. He asked for directions to the nearest inn, and began leading his horse in that direction. Whenever his steed seemed to be walking quietly enough to require only one hand for guidance, Flutirr would let his free hand toy with the hilt of his sword. It was only the feel of this cold metal against his skin and the comforting *clump* of his heavy dragon-leather boots on the stone road that kept him from feeling alien and naked.

Later that evening, Flutirr sat in an Elvin inn with

an empty plate before him and a hot drink cradled in his hands. Wearily, he sat back. Once again, his flute music had been popular with the other guests of the inn—indeed, it seemed his music was becoming more and more popular the longer Flutirr traveled and the more he experimented with unNoblish music. Right now, however, Flutirr cared only about finishing his drink and going upstairs to sleep, so he could escape the eyes of all the guests in the inn who were seeing him without his cape.

An Elvin guest plopped down in the chair across the table from Flutirr and promptly fell into a thoughtful reverie, completely ignoring the room about him. Flutirr had originally been astonished at the number of Elvins to be found in the inns of Elvin villages—he had assumed any inn would surely contain mostly people of other races. Instead, it seemed Elvins traveled more than any other race. Elvin traders actively exported and imported materials to and from other Elvin villages, and it was these traders who commonly filled Elvin inns. It was the traders of all races who had proved to be the most likely to lay claim to knowing of the Hijj. It was an almost automatic reaction for Flutirr to lean forward and ask, "Are you a trader?"

The Elvin glanced at him and paused for half a moment before answering, as though he needed to remind himself that there was someone sitting across the table from him. "Yes. So I am."

"And you travel a lot? You have heard many tales of other races?"

"Like any trader—yes."

"Then—have you heard of the Hijj?"

The Elvin shifted his position, and looked at Flutirr more alertly than before. "Heard of them? I have seen them!"

"You—" Flutirr was startled into speechlessness. He had long ago stopped hoping to meet someone like this Elvin. He had expected only to obtain more hearsay information that might permit him to cull a few more clues about where he ought to be heading and how much farther he should go. "You—so you—so you know where they are then? You know how I can find them?"

"Tell me, my dear Nelvin—would you be seeking information on these Hijj?"

"I have just indicated that." Had Flutirr's Elvinese been that poor?

"How vital is this information to you? Why do you need to find these Hijj?"

Why would this Elvin want to know? "I am seeking a cure for Sporadasm. I was told that these Hijj might be able to give me one."

"Sporadasm? The syllables are familiar to me, but I do not recognize the illness. A Nelvin disease, is it?"

Flutirr was momentarily flustered: Sporadasm was one of the most well-known illnesses among Nelvins. Flutirr had never considered the fact that an Elvin would not have heard of it. "Yes. Always a fatal one, and not as rare as it should be."

"Forgive me, my dear Nelvin—I have traded only

a little with your race, and have not learned all I could of your kind. I am from far away in the west, and have had little reason to travel to the Centre of Nelvins I have heard of in the east. Nevertheless, if Sporadasm is as common as you say, then the Hijj would surely know of a cure. All herbs are known to them, as well as the effects of all possible combinations of all possible plants.

"But tell me—for whom are you trying to obtain this cure? For a lover, perhaps? A lover with tender black eyes, and long glossy hair who lies at home waiting? But I see from your blank look, my dear Nelvin, that I am incorrect. So it must be another loved one—perhaps a relative, a young child of yours? But I had forgotten—you Nelvins marry late in life, do you not? Surely you would not have children already. So you desire the cure for a friend?"

"An acquaintance," Flutirr said curtly.

"Indeed? Then you must enjoy challenge and hardship if you would journey such a great distance and gamble so much on the kindness of the Hijj for a mere acquaintance. For surely you have heard of the Hijj's harsh nature and the difficulty of persuading a Hijj to do your will. But come, my dear Nelvin. Let me not concern you with such things. It is time to establish—the terms."

"The terms—"

"Of our agreement, my dear Nelvin! Didn't you know that a trader must trade for everything? Did you expect me to speak for free?"

"But—I have nothing to trade!"

"Those shoes on your feet—they seem quite fine to me."

Flutirr was horrified. Surely the Elvin trader could not be seriously proposing that he give up his dragon-leather boots to—

The look in the Elvin's eyes said that he was utterly serious. Flutirr faltered. He couldn't give up his most treasured possession—yet he also couldn't keep searching for the Hijj by following rumors. What if he was headed in the wrong direction? This Elvin could save him countless days of precious time—if Flutirr paid his price.

Yet his dragon-leather boots . . .

"Or, if you would rather, the sword you carry at your waist would be a valuable addition to my collection."

Flutirr released a huff of breath in relief. Better his sword than his boots.

The Elvin gave a small, smug smile. "My dear Nelvin. I take it you are amenable. Have you seen the mountains that are approaching from the west?" Flutirr nodded. He had first seen a collection of mountain peaks peering over the horizon just the previous day. "It is three days of traveling until you reach those mountains, then three days more until you are through the mountain range. There, almost instantly, will be the Land of the Hijj. You may have been told of a clear path through the mountains that is a little to the north. You must not take that path, or you will miss the Hijj."

This was valuable information indeed. Earlier that

evening, two guests of the inn had independently mentioned that very path. Without hearing this new information, he would have used it.

Grudgingly, Flutirr surrendered his sword and went up the stairs to find his room. As he prepared himself for sleep, his hands rose automatically to his neck—but of course his cape was no longer there to be removed. His hands lowered automatically to his waist—but of course his sword was no longer there, either. There was only the flute, water bottle, and money bag to be removed. And the dragon-leather boots.

He sat on his sleeping mattress for a long time, holding his boots. They were the only possessions left that could remind Flutirr of his High Noble status. He must never give them up.

Flutirr put his boots on the ground and lay in such a position that he could still see his boots. They would be the last image to burn into his eyeballs before sleep, and the first to greet him when he woke.

No. He could never give them up.

Chapter 15

A<small>T</small> last! At last, the mountains! The glorious mountains that ate half the sky above him, the wondrous mountains that greeted his eyes when Flutirr woke!

After the initial waking euphoria, Flutirr's more cynical, Noblish side asserted itself. There were still three days more of hard travel before him, he reminded himself, so it was not quite yet the halfway point of his journey. Even if he were to turn about this moment and head home, Don might still be dead by the time he arrived. Sporadasm, it was true, normally took two Thunderballs or, on rare occasions, even three to complete its course. Don had not even entered the delirium stage, much less the stage of spasms and seizures, when Flutirr had left him. Still, Don was underfed and therefore weak; any illness was likely to progress faster in such a situation.

Flutirr hesitated in mounting his mare, seeing Don before him again. Don, huddled under a pile of blankets on the bare ground, so withered and thin his form could not be detected among them. Don, speaking as tartly as ever, yet fully aware of his impending death, of the impending fevers that would plunge him into delirium off and on for Dewlights until the end. Don with the lisp who was not afraid to speak even the words his lips had to struggle to express. Don, who played the flute to greet the dawn; where was that flute now—collecting dust in a corner? Don now most likely either in a delirium or dreaming ghostly dreams between fits. Don, dying.

What a fool he had been, Flutirr cursed himself, believing he could do anything just because he was a Noble. What could he, Noble or no Noble, possibly do to ensure that Don would actually live until Flutirr returned, with or without a cure? Why had he believed that the solution was as simple as mounting a horse at dawn and searching for someone with all the answers, as if such a creature existed?

Flutirr literally shuddered all over for a moment; perhaps it was a message from the depths of his subconscious to tell him to begin, to mount his horse, for it was dawn and the mountains were waiting.

He pushed his thoughts aside. Nobles did not think such things. Nobles never considered even the possibility of failure. Nothing bad could ever occur as long as a High Noble was there to handle it.

With his back to the sun, he hoisted himself onto his mount—he must create a name for her sometime, he thought absently—and began to pick his way up and over the first mountain.

* * *

Mountains, mountains, and mountains. They reached above him to frightening heights. He only hoped the near-invisible paths he followed would not lead him over too many of them. The mountains also spread below him, reminding him repeatedly of how high he was already—higher than any Nelvin had a right to be. Nelvins were made for flat country that nuts grew on, not for ground that swept up and down like a bouncing globe of rubber he had seen a child playing with in that Human village, or like that queer wooden toy in one of those Elvin towns that was made of two sticks and a wooden sphere that had to be bounced between them in increasingly higher arches without touching the ground.

Sometimes the slope was so gentle it was like walking through a field. Sometimes Flutirr had to dismount his horse and cautiously lead her over the steep ground, and all but carry her up to the next ledge. At these times Flutirr wondered if perhaps he shouldn't have left her behind somewhere so she wouldn't be slowing him down now. But then mealtime would come, and he would dig gratefully into the food supply his mare carried for him. Flutirr would never have been able to carry all the supplies he needed by himself.

The nights were almost sleepless, in part from anticipation, and in part because he had a fear of tumbling down the mountain. There were creatures, he had heard, who actually made their homes in the mountains. He believed it, of course, but how in Nobleness's name did anyone other than fairies and other flying creatures ever find the nerve to stay more than a day or two on these things?

He climbed over and around perhaps a half dozen mountains in three days. There was nothing but more mountains.

What if the Elvin trader had known nothing and had only invented a tale to please him, to cheat his sword away from him? Could it be that the creatures Flutirr had spent the last three Dewlights searching for did not even exist? What if he was, by some horrendous accident, only traveling deeper into the mountain range and not across it?

No, the last could not be so, for he was at all times careful to keep the sun to his back in the morning and ahead of him in the afternoon, right where it belonged. But either of the first two possibilities could well be true. Or perhaps the Elvin had only underestimated the distance, not accounting for the difficulties his mare would provide.

He pressed onward, and found yet more mountains before him. On the eighth day he came upon what he thought must be the highest mountain of the range. He searched for a way to pass it, but could not find a way: on either side were thick bushes of thorns, which he had found through painful experience were the type that hid stinging insects. If he wanted to get to the other side, he would have to climb this mountain.

Easier, he thought despairingly, to give up on the whole journey and go home.

Still, what was one more mountain? One more day?

Perhaps he would be able to see something from the summit. Seeing no way to scale the slope while mounted, he climbed to the ground and tried to trace a path up the face that would take both Nelvin and horse.

The face, in turn, glared hostilely back at him. Every possible path he could see led to a place where he, perhaps, could climb by grasping and pulling with his hands, but his mare could not. Perhaps a more experienced mountain climber could have found a way; he could not.

His mare would have to stay behind.

And he hadn't, Flutirr thought in passing, even made a name for her.

He relieved her of her various burdens and looked through them carefully to choose what he could afford to bring and what he could not. Food, of course, he took. The cloak he needed for chilly nights, and he could tie it at the four corners to use for a bag, so he took that too. With the cloak, the bags wouldn't be needed anymore, so he took only one in case a need arose for it and left the rest. Both of the blankets he had had once had been pawned somewhere, so they were not there to be taken. The rope had mainly been used to help his mare up and down the mountains, and it was one of his heaviest possessions, so he left it behind. Horse feed, naturally, was now senseless to bring along. The only clothes he had left were those he wore.

What else was there? The flute he needed to earn his living. The sword and cape were, of course, now gone. The boots had to stay with him since he had nothing else to cover his feet, and, of course, he could not sacrifice his sole remaining Noblish possession. Money bag, pants, shirt, belt, food, water in water bottle, flute, cloak.

Oh yes, here was that little clay figurine that young Elvin child had clumsily thrust at him just before he had left her home. He had been made to understand that she was deaf, and could barely hear the spoken voice let alone understand it. Yet she had seemed to need nothing more than for him to repeat himself a few times for her to follow him and his awkward Elvinese. She was, her parents explained, watching the movements of his lips to understand him. Her speech, the parents added, had been obtained through years of feeling vibrations at the throat and the flow of air at the mouth, and through using the tiny portion of hearing she did have at her command. It was enough hearing, he noted, to give her some pleasure in listening to and watching him play the flute. She had enjoyed him so much her hands spontaneously blurred through the air in that odd Language of the Fingers she and her family had created for easier communication. That night, after Flutirr went to sleep, she had made a clay figurine that was clearly intended to resemble him as he played the flute. But of course it was not a precise likeness; the look on his face was too gentle, too kind, too enraptured by the message he was trying to draw from his soul and through his flute, to be anything like Flutirr at all. It was too unNoblish a picture of him to be true, and should have been thrown out weeks ago.

So why did he feel such a pang at the moment he realized it was too heavy and bulky to bring along?

He removed his mare's bridle and her saddle and sent her on her way. He would worry about paying for her loss when he returned home; technically, he was only renting her. She might even arrive before him, for she was walking toward Trilene. Animals, he had heard, had good instincts, especially the kind that led one home. This steed, he knew, was a clever creature who ought to be able to locate food and water when she needed it.

Ironic, Flutirr thought, that he had sacrificed his cape rather than incurring future expense by selling his rented mare—and now he was losing her after all.

Flutirr started, at last, after the noon meal.

There was only the stone: the stone that his knees insisted on bumping against each time he pulled himself up another inch; the stone that refused to help him find any handholds; the stone that found its way under his fingernails, into his hair, even into his nostrils and his mouth, in the form of dust and tiny coarse pebbles. But he did not yet despair, despite the soreness his neck suffered from the weight of the cloakbag he carried on his back. He did not yet despair, despite the blood he thought he saw on his hands—he couldn't even check because his hands needed to be above him reaching for the next handhold, not down by his eyes for his eyes to see. He did not despair, for just up there was what seemed to be a ledge, a resting place, a goal for him to work toward.

Foot by foot, sometimes inch by inch, he aimed himself toward the ledge with sweating, bleeding hands (yes, they were bleeding, he could see that now). He arrived at the ledge by early evening— except there was no ledge. Certainly nothing wide enough for him to rest on. It had only been an aberration all along, a funny curve in the stone that had seemed to hide more than it did. He had more climbing to do.

Sweat made his clothes as wet as if he had been drenched by a waterfall, even now when the sun was almost ready to set, no longer draining the water from his body. He suspected he was bleeding even more than before, but he could not stop to check. He was certain that his pants were being worn to their last thread, and his shirt was receiving similar treatment. The boots, at least, were sturdy enough to hold up, and he hardly seemed to be using his feet anyway. Darkness began to tinge the air, but the ledge he was now heading toward still seemed far away.

The sun was clearly setting now, and Flutirr wished he were on the ground to witness it as he had the past few nights he had spent among the mountains. The darkness about him deepened to the kind of shade that makes one look about and say, "Yes, it is dark," and is yet just light enough that one could recognize a friend from a small distance if there were a friend present to be recognized.

Flutirr squinted to make out the shape of the rocks ahead of him and only then noticed that he had been squinting a while now just to see where he was. What if he were to be trapped here until morning by the indestructible enemy of night? Something got into his eyes, and they watered so badly that tears momentarily streamed down his cheek. Nobleness dash the dust, he thought, but did not say for he no longer had the breath. He climbed onward out of fear that he would fall asleep and fall to—he didn't want to think about such things. He had to climb onward lest his muscles cramp overnight and make it impossible for him to move without endangering himself. He climbed wholly by touch now, and only then realized he had been going more by the feel of the stones than by sight all along. He prayed to an unknown entity that he was moving in the right direction.

The moons rose to help him locate his new ledge again. Yes, thank Nobleness, it *was* a ledge, thank Nobleness, it was. Thank High Nobleness, thank the Highest Nobleness, a ledge. Flutirr climbed.

Flutirr climbed, one hand over the other, pull-himself-up-pray-the-bag-of-precious-ohsoprecious-supplies-doesn't-fall—and start over again, with his feet scrabbling under him for a place to rest, searching for those handholds he remembered from just a moment before, hours ago, an infinity ago. And here, here was the ledge, and here was two hours of sleep before dawn.

* * *

The sun passed over him so gently he did not wake until mid-morning. Only then did he inspect his scrapes and scratches from the day before. They were almost as bad as he had thought, but he did not have nearly enough water either to wash his injuries or to ease the sunburn he was getting. That would have to wait until he found a river. For now, now he had more climbing to do, perhaps another half day's worth just to reach the summit.

He ate his meal and began.

His hands ached, his knees ached, his elbows and shoulders and neck and even the skin that was long overexposed to the sun were all burning with pain. The only thing that kept his cheeks from cracking with dryness were the dust-disturbed tears streaming from his eyes.

The summit.

Now he could drink, but only a sip for there was not much water left. Now he could eat, but only a bite for there was not much food left either. Now he could rest, but not for long, for he still needed to reach the ground.

Now, to look about him and see: was there anything here, anything at all?

Mountains. Trees. A little glitter of the type a lake or river would make. And the sky and the clouds and no Land of the Hijj.

It was time to turn about and go home, to go home to his mother and his father and his school and his classes, tests, and homework. Time to go home to nuts, sauces, and Nelvin spices.

And to Don, who was going to die, because even a Noble had failed to help him.

Dust got in his eyes again, but he had become accustomed to letting the tears stream without wiping them away, so he did nothing.

He made another halfhearted search. Mountains, trees, and that little glitter again that reminded him of the roofs at the Dwaline village he had stayed at. Even from a distance, the Dwaline roofs had reflected the sunlight to him, and it had been hours before he had discovered the cause.

Roofs?

No, it was foolish to think of it as anything other than a lake.

He climbed down the mountain and headed toward the glint of light that had called to him on the summit.

Chapter 16

FLUTIRR flung his head back and coaxed just a little more water onto his tongue. A few drops trickled out of his water bottle—then no more.

No, that was wrong, he wasn't that low, he *couldn't* be that low. He had rationed himself: first three mouthfuls a day, then two, then one, then a single stingy sip at noon.

Wearily, he hung the empty water bottle at his belt. If that glitter he had seen two days before was only a lake after all, then at least he would get to drink.

Light-headed with hunger, thirst, and exhaustion, he pushed onward. Soon it was night, so Flutirr lay on the ground and slept. He dreamed. He dreamed of Don dreaming, of nightmare hallucinations sent by Sporadasm dancing before his eyes. Don, screaming for someone—no, only crying, speaking in an incoherent wail. Don, flailing his arms until someone with a gentle touch comes to tend to him.

"Shhh, Don, drink this."

He drinks a few sips, and immediately spits the

rancid potion from his mouth. Somewhere, there is a voice gently urging him—he must take his medicine, it may help . . .

But this is wrong. He is not Don, he is Flutirr. And Don cannot be taking medicine now because there is no medicine for Sporadasm. It is for this medicine that he has come searching for the Hijj—

Then Flutirr was awake, but the tendrils of his dream seemed to be lingering: he was in a gray plain, and the gray was swirling, blending with green and blue. Here, now, was grass; here, now, was sky. And standing, towering over him, were three men standing side by side. Too startled to speak, Flutirr simply lay still. One of the men stepped forward.

"——————," he said in a language utterly alien to Flutirr. Then, seeing Flutirr's incomprehension, he spoke in heavily accented Elvinese: "We are the Hijj."

The Hijj! Flutirr scrambled to his feet. "I—I am Sinie-Tilll. My acquaintance, Don, he needs medicine . . . he has Sporadasm. I was told to come here."

"You must speak again. My Elvinese is poor, for I have learned only a little from the few Elvin traders who have come here." Flutirr spoke again, with less of the agitation that had sped and blurred his speech before. This time the Hijj understood, and said: "Yes. Many who come here have asked us to grant our medicines for various ills. But it is not mine to decide. You must direct your request and your defense to the Council. Come, and we will take you to the village."

Flutirr hastily gathered his things as the Hijj turned and left him. The Hijj were already far ahead of him when he was able to follow—they were even taller than Humans, and walked at a faster pace as well. For a moment, Flutirr thought he had lost the Hijj among the trees, then he found the threesome again. And here, at last, was the tiny Hijj village: a collection of a few dozen wooden buildings, each with a roof made of some strange substance that glittered in the sun.

The three Hijj men conferred with one another before two of them left and vanished among the houses. The third turned to Flutirr and said: "Come. I will take you to the place where you shall meet the Council. I shall teach you our ways, for you must not greet the Council with the same rudeness you met us. The Council is far less understanding of outsiders than I." The Hijj swept away so swiftly Flutirr had no chance to ask his bewildered question of what rudeness he could have possibly committed during his brief, harmless encounter with the Hijj trio. Instead, he could only scoop up the bag he had lowered to the ground and once again follow at an unNoblishly undignified trot.

"Wait, you Hijj!" Couldn't the infernal creature at least turn around and acknowledge him? "Wait!" Flutirr was led to the opposite end of the small village and into a tiny clearing a dozen steps into the forest. There wasn't even a path to the clearing; his less-than-secure grip on his bags was momentarily threatened when he stumbled into a bush. The Hijj—who had now arrived in the clearing, and was watching him—never once offered assistance.

"You Hijj! Didn't you see that I had these bags to carry? And haven't you learned the common courtesy of offering a drink of water to your guests before you lead them at a dragon's pace straight through un-Noblish bushes like these?"

"I will once again forgive your rudeness, for you are only an ignorant Nelvin—but I shall not answer questions that so glaringly show how little you know of our ways. Be seated, Sinie-Tilll, and we can begin the teaching." The hostile pair settled onto the ground, watching each other warily. "Sinie-Tilll. You have liberally given us the gift of your name. This forces me to give you my name as well, though I offer it not in honor of any bond between us but to ease the gift-stigma of your name. My name is Keej."

"Keej," Flutirr said, then shifted uncomfortably at his stomach's hungry growling. "But—"

"*Silence,* Sinie-Tilll! I am here to teach you, not to hear you prattle." The Hijj glared Flutirr into acquiescence. "I offer you my teaching in honor of the bond you and I possess between us by being born from the same sky and by dying to enter the same earth. And know, Sinie-Tilll, that I can dare to put the burden of so big a gift on so weak a bond only because my two companions have permitted me to use this teaching to ease the gift-stigma you put on them by granting your name in the improper manner.

"Let this be your first lesson, Sinie-Tilll—that even as small a gift as a name must be offered in honor of some bond between two persons, however tenuous that bond. When a gift is given in honor of the wrong kind of bond, or in honor of no bond at all, then a gift-stigma is put on both giver and receiver. If you had come to our people a mere century ago and put the same gift-stigma on yourself and the three of us, then all four of us would have had to suffer a cleansing process I am sure you would not have enjoyed, Sinie-Tilll. Your demand for assistance and water was an improper one—you have yet to cross the threshold to my home, and so no host-guest bond exists between us. I can offer you nothing more than the teaching I am granting you now.

"This lesson is a vital one to recall when you greet the Council. When you greet them, you must offer your name in honor of the bond you share by being born of the same sky and by dying to enter the same earth. That is the only bond you possess with anyone on the Council, and the only one you may use. When you have given the gift of your name, then you may make your request.

"You, Sinie-Tilll, come to us seeking a gift. The Council does not look lightly upon one who expects them to take gift-stigma upon themselves. Two generations of Elvin traders frequenting the village, however, have slowly taught us the wisdom of occasionally easing a gift-stigma by granting a gift of equal value in return. It has allowed us a generation of trade, once our Council was fully convinced the new practice was wise; we trade our medicines for the Elvin herbs we cannot obtain in the forest that surrounds us. If you have a question you may ask it.''

Flutirr hesitated a moment to formulate a question out of the swirl of new information the Hijj had force-fed him. Who could have conceived of a society so tangled with mysterious rituals concerning bonds and gifts that as small an act as uttering one's name without the proper ceremony was taboo?

''Keej—would the Council accept a few days of labor and a few hours of hearing me play the flute in exchange for medicine? I have no herbs.''

''The only labor you could do for us is labor we do not need. As for your flute, Sinie-Tilll, none of the Hijj would want to fritter away time listening to tedious noise when we could be using the time to work. No, Sinie-Tilll—the only gifts I have ever seen the Council accept are the rarest of herbs for the various potions and medicines made by the villagers. The Council would have no interest in any gifts of luxury you might have to offer.''

Flutirr felt a trickle of panicked despair. Had he come all this way only to fail because of these stringent Hijjian customs that left no room for compassion? ''But then—how am I to get the medicine?''

''If you do not carry any herbs, then you must be able to lay valid claim to some bond so strong it demands honor even from Hijj to whom you are a stranger.''

''You just said that I have only a weak bond of earth and sky with the Council. What other bond could I possibly claim?''

"Sinie-Tilll." Keej made a noise that sounded suspiciously like a stifled groan of impatience. "Sinie-Tilll, gifts do no always have to be given in honor of bonds between the giver and receiver. It is a Hijjian tradition, for instance, for the whole village to build a new house in honor of a newly formed mating bond—even if many of the builders have no more than an acquaintance bond with either of the new couple. But silence, Sinie-Tilll—the Council comes."

The sound of distant feet slapping against hard ground that Flutirr had been hearing the past few moments faded into the rustle of bushes. Eight robed men appeared. One of them stepped forward and spoke in Elvinese that was less accented than that of Keej. "We are the Council. You have a request you would make of us. You may stand and speak of it."

Flutirr stood. He almost asked where their women were, for it was odd that any Council of this size should be missing representatives of half their population. But no—these were ferocious-looking men with long, white beards and faces with harsh, stubborn lines that seemed never to have known a smile. They did not seem the sort to tolerate any questions of idle curiosity.

"I—I offer my name in honor of the bond we share by being born of the same sky and by dying into the same earth. My request is for a supply of whatever medicine you may possess that could cure the Nelvin illness of Sporadasm." There. That was the first step. Now he had to find some bond in his life that the Council would willingly honor.

"You request a gift, and name no bond that this gift would honor. Are you, then, a Nelvin trader come to trade some valuable herb for our medicine? If so, name your herb."

"I do not have a herb—I am not even a trader. I need the medicine for a Nelvin who is ill."

"Is your intention to put gift-stigma upon us?"

"No! I—I ask that this gift be given in honor of my bond with my parents." If Nelvins were to put as much value on bonds between each other as these Hijj did, then it would surely be the parent-child bond that would be considered the strongest. Would the Hijj Council think the same?

"Is it, then, one of your parents who is ill?"

"No, not a parent—an acquain—a friend of mine."

"If it is indeed a friend of yours who is ill, then where is your bonding wound?"

"Bonding wound? I don't understand—"

"The bonding wound of your friendship! Are Nelvins so woefully backward that they do not teach their own children about bonding wounds?" Flutirr would have stammered some incoherent response to the accusation if one of the seven Councilmen behind the spokesman had not moved forward.

"Sinie-Tilll," the new Councilman said, "the ritual of bonding is performed to show that love and friendship runs so deep one values the blood of the other more than one's own. Each friend uses a knife to draw blood from his own body, and in that way, the friends are bonded to each other for life. A bonding wound is almost like a mating wound; this is the scar I bear from my first mating." The Councilman pulled back his long sleeve. Now Flutirr could see the long, pale scar that ran from his elbow to his wrist. He shuddered. How could these Hijj see this barbaric practice as a way to express friendship? The sleeve settled back into place, and the Councilman stepped back.

"I have no bonding wound."

"No bonding wound? You would dare suggest first that we honor your parent-child bond when neither parent is ill, then that we honor your friendship bond when you do not even consider the friendship to be of sufficient strength to be worthy of a bonding wound? You ask gift-stigma of us!"

"No, wait—among Nelvins—"

"Enough! You shall not receive the medicine!"

The effect of the Hijj's words was like a bolt of wild lightning leaping out of nowhere, paralyzing Flutirr where he stood—he could not react when the Council turned as one unit and left the clearing.

Flutirr would not receive the medicine. He had traveled a Thunderball away from his parents, his school, and his home—and now he was to travel another Thunderball back again, with nothing to show for his travels. He had failed.

And Don was going to die.

"Keej—can't you—they don't understand—Nelvins have never—"

"There is nothing that can be done, Sinie-Till. Those on the Council are the oldest in the village. They remember our people the way we were before the first Elvin traders came to us two generations ago, and know no other way. They have learned the ancient Elvin tongue that has been passed down from parent to child for over a thousand years since our people first knew isolation, and they have learned more of the modern tongue in recent decades. The cures for the illnesses known to every species of the land of Trillilani have been passed down as well, along with a description of the appearances and the ways of each of those species. Still, it seems incomprehensible to most of the Council that anyone would not know of, or not want to follow, the Hijjian ways. Only the youngest, who spoke to you of his mating wound, is more enlightened. It is quite regrettable that the only thing you had to offer for the medicine was a friendship bond that could not be proved by Hijjian customs—but that cannot be helped."

"But—Don—"

"Don will die. You are to be my guest tonight. Come."

For a moment, it had seemed that Keej, at least, understood—and now this bluntness. Flutirr numbly followed. Keej led him to his home near the center of the village. Flutirr idly reached up to touch the strange, shiny roof of Keej's hut, but it was too far above him. It looked like it might be metal—but who would use so much metal for a single roof, when there were other things to be made with such valuable substance?

"Enter, Sinie-Tilll, and let us be bonded as host and guest." Flutirr crossed the threshold into the one-room hut; the accomodations seemed quite rude compared to the mansion that served as his home in Trilene, but pleasantly comfortable compared to some of the inns Flutirr had had to stay at during his journey. Compared to Don's hut, it was positively—

Flutirr tried not to think of Don.

"Keej, what is this?"

Keej looked where Flutirr was pointing. A slim, gracefully curved knife with a smoky gray handle hung on one wall of the hut. It was clear that the blade had been finely honed—yet the knife seemed more a work of art than a weapon. "That is a juunkik. I made it myself. Would you like to hear more about it?"

Perhaps a little conversation would keep his mind too busy to think of his failure that day. "Yes."

"Then bring it here, for it is time to eat. I offer you my food and my water, in honor of our host-guest bond." Flutirr cautiously removed the knife from the wall and did as he was asked. He spent the first few moments of the meal, however, doing nothing but eating and drinking. The oddness of the food did not even make him hesitate—a huge mushroom was served on his plate, stuffed with some unidentifiable creamy substance that had the tangy taste of berries and the dry texture of flour. Flutirr had not even known that mushrooms could be edible. Only when his hunger and thirst had both been somewhat satiated did he begin to slow.

"You have been hungry, Sinie-Tilll."

"Yes. I have only a few bites of food left, and I ran out of water altogether just yesterday."

"Then you found us just in time. But let me tell you about the juunkik." Keej promptly launched into a prolonged monologue, describing the history of the juunkik, and the methods he had used to shape the metal and polish the handle. Slowly, the gruff, taciturn man he had been faded away to be replaced by an animated being, in love with his art. "And, Sinie-Tilll," he said, well into his lecture, "the most difficult part was the pictures on the blade. Can you see them in this light?" Now that the Hijj had brought them to his attention, Flutirr could indeed see the shadowy shape of a woman on one side of the blade and the equally mysterious form of a man on the other. The pictures had been formed in shallow bas-relief, and made economical use of the entire surface of the blade. The simple eloquence of the lines was jarring; Flutirr had not expected such tenderness from a race that seemed so harsh.

"Yes—they are beautiful."

The Hijj responded with a detailed description of how he had created the pictures. The hard lines of his face seemed to have melted away in an eerily familiar passion.

Flutirr was reminded of Don, sitting by the river, telling him what he thought of music. And now, Don would not be able to play his music anymore; he would not be able to play songs about the sun, or about birds, or about golden reeds.

"*Sinie-Tilll!* Do you not hear me? I asked if something in what I say disturbs you?"

"Wh—no."

"Then perhaps something puzzles you. If you have a question, you may ask it."

"I—I was wondering—what is the purpose of a juunkik? Decoration?"

Keej looked as though Flutirr had asked if the Hijj practiced cannibalism. "No true Hijj would produce an item just for frivolous decoration! This is the knife my mate and I used to form our mating bond!"

Flutirr had been admiring a work of art that had drawn blood.

"You needn't look with disgust, Sinie-Tilll. An Elvin trader once told me of Nelvins and the swords many of them carry. Am I to believe you never use those swords? Or that a sword is any better than a juunkik?"

"That isn't the same," he said. But the Hijj had made him stop to think. A Noble sword was only drawn in violence, or to assert authority. One did not simply wound with a sword—one killed. A juunkik, at least, would never kill—and it was used to bind two people together, if rather brutally, in love. Flutirr looked again at the blade he still held idly in his hand. To put such beauty into a juunkik showed these Hijj saw beauty in the ceremony of making a mating wound. And for an instant, Flutirr could almost see as the Hijj saw: two lovers embracing, each sacrificing some of his or her own blood for the other—the blood mingling, the two lovers unified—

Or two friends.

Flutirr thought again of Don—but, of course, the idea was unthinkable. It would not be honest. They were not really friends. They had barely had time to get to know each other—

In his mind's eye, he saw Don as he had stood in the moonlight that long-ago night, silently studying Flutirr—Flutirr, the Noble who had invaded Don's territory, and threatened Don's life, then conceded to him. Don's steady gaze seemed to make a dare. *Do something.*

It was too late, Flutirr thought in protest. And, besides, Don was a classless one—Flutirr could not—

The words seemed feeble to Flutirr's ear.

Do something.

"Keej—would the Council hear a request from me a second time?"

"I have never seen them do so with any Elvin trader. I am certain they would hear you only if you had some new thing to offer."

"Like a bonding wound?"

For once, the Hijj seemed to be speechless. Then he bowed his head and said: "Forgive me, Sinie-Tilll. I have misjudged you. I had known for a long time that one not raised to our ways would not know of them or follow them—but I had always thought of other races as being too inferior to learn Hijjian ways. Yes, I think that, perhaps, a bonding wound would make the Council listen to you again. Wait—I shall fetch a more appropriate knife." He rummaged through some boxes in a corner and returned with a knife similar in shape to the juunkik, but made with a plain blade. "This is a juunikik that has never been used. It is impossible to do the ceremony properly without your friend, but if you make your wound deep enough it may not matter to the Council. You must say: *I invoke friendship*, then cut from here to here on your left arm." Keej traced a path from the inside of his own elbow to the inside of his wrist. "Take care not to let your knife slip—you will not be cutting far from a major vein."

Flutirr took the knife and tugged his sleeve up his arm with trembling hands. He had committed himself now—he could not turn back. He had to do it for Don—for his friend.

"I invoke friendship," he said, and put the cold blade on the naked skin of his arm, ready to cut. He would do it quickly, then it would be over before he knew it. It was simply a matter of telling his hand to move.

Move!

His hand kept twitching away—he was too afraid to do it. He shouldn't have even thought of such an insane notion. No, it was best to give up.

"Perhaps you are not truly worthy of your friend. If you wish, I can take the knife away," Keej said.

Not worthy? His pride wounded, Flutirr gulped a breath of air, squeezed his eyes shut, and tried again—

And so he did it. He did it, then the knife fell from his hand as he clutched his searing arm in agony. He had *done* it.

Keej was abruptly by his side, cleansing his wound with cold, soothing water. "I do not think even the eldest, most orthodox Council member could deny a bonding wound as deep as this. You are sure to receive the medicine. And I, in honor of your friendship bond, shall give you a gift from me. I am a teacher in the village—I can teach you to make the medicine for yourself, so you can share this teaching with the Nelvins of your home.''

This would be a gift even more valuable than the medicine itself. Hundreds of Nelvins would be saved each year from Sporadasm—and thousands more during an epidemic. "I—I thank you," Flutirr said.

Keej finished bandaging Flutirr's arm in silence, then said: "Wait. I shall fetch the Council again." He left the hut.

Tentatively, Flutirr touched the bandage that covered his bonding wound. His whole arm throbbed with pain, but somehow it didn't matter. Flutirr would get the medicine now. He was going home. There was still hope for Don.

Chapter 17

THREE days later, Flutirr frowned into his newly replenished supply bag. The Hijj had given him two weeks' worth of food. It was a generous amount, but Flutirr had been hoping for more. With careful rationing, and by earning his meals at each village he stopped at, the food could last perhaps a full third of a Thunderball at the most. After that, he would have to pawn something—and he had nothing left to pawn. It was a serious dilemma—it had taken him nearly a full Thunderball to reach the Hijj, and would surely take even longer to return home without his mare to ride.

Well, it was no good worrying about such things before they occurred. Flutirr closed his supply bag, hefted it onto his shoulder, favoring his still-sore arm, and headed toward home. As Flutirr had predicted, his supplies vanished rapidly during his trip through the mountains. By the time he returned to civilization, most of his food had been consumed—and what he had lasted little more than a week after that. He *had* to pawn something.

Flutirr stubbornly raised his jaw. He would *not*. He was now in an Elvin village, and the next source of food was four or five days away—but a few days of hunger would not hurt him. Flutirr plunged back into the wilderness. Perhaps he would find a solution at the next village.

The next village was a village of Kuu. By the time Flutirr arrived, his stomach was growling almost continually, and he was certain he was feeling more and more of his bones through his skin every day. He would be able to play his flute for a meal tonight— but one complete meal would not be enough to fill him up and also tide him over during his next stretch in the wilderness. He had to do something about his situation.

After a few minutes of searching, he found the bazaar section of town. There, he found a merchant of clothes—a middle-aged woman with gray blended into her brown hair, who watched Flutirr curiously as he approached. She launched into her sales pitch, speaking in fluent Elvinese, before Flutirr could say one word.

"You, handsome Nelvin! Won't you come look at my fine clothes to replace the ones you wear? I have clothes at all prices, for all budgets! And I even have large pieces of clothing for large Nelvins like you!"

"Your honorness, I wish to pawn these clothes for Ku money and cheaper clothes."

The Ku merchant let her mouth gape a moment in open astonishment, then she broke into a high-pitched peal of laughter. "I did not think that anyone wearing such boots as those could be so poor! Those clothes are cheaper than anything I sell, my dear—I simply cannot accept them.''

For a moment, Flutirr's hand twitched, as though reaching to fondle the hilt of a sword that was no longer there. The merchants of Trilene were never so blatantly rude or insulting even to clients of the lowest classes. "If you will not accept these clothes, then I will need directions to a merchant who will."

"Your honorness, the only thing you are wearing that anyone would buy are your boots. No one wants clothes as filthy and worn as yours."

Flutirr cast about for alternatives. "What about my flute?"

"Oh, Great Sky! I certainly don't know of any Kuu who have seen Nelvinese flutes more than once or twice, let alone learned how to play them. It would be a foolish merchant indeed who buys your flute with hopes to sell it at a profit. There's only your boots, unless you have something better in that bag you carry on your back."

There was nothing. There were only the herbs he needed for Don's medicine—

The herbs. Mightn't they have some value? Wouldn't the ready-made medicine he carried be sufficient for Don? If he searched hard enough in the wilderness, wouldn't he be able to replace the herbs later?

Flutirr flinched at a sudden wave of shame. These were the herbs, the medicine, the formula he had traveled over a Thunderball to obtain. They were for

Don. Don, the friend to whom he had bonded himself.

Don. If Flutirr starved himself to death, or even slowed himself down to ease the agitation of a hungry stomach, then Don could die. Die because Flutirr did not want to sell his boots. Die because Flutirr would rather retain his boots than survive.

Flutirr could not afford to think only of himself, or what sacrifices he was willing to make in order to cling to his boots. When he made a choice, he was making a decision for Don as well as for himself. He was endangering Don's life for two inanimate objects that did no more than adorn Flutirr's feet and let him call himself a High Noble.

"I—I will sell these boots. How much would you buy them for?"

The Ku merchant leaned forward to get a better view of Flutirr's boots. Then she said: "If you'd take this cloth, my dear—there's so much mud on those things I can't possibly see what they're worth." Flutirr took the cloth and cleaned his boots. Then the Ku said: "Come closer. Let me see better." Flutirr obeyed that also, feeling for a moment as though he himself was the object to be sold. At last the Ku said: "I will buy them for fifty thousand Rublins."

How much would that be in Jublas? Flutirr tangled himself into some complicated calculations based on the price of Ku supplies he had bought at previous villages, and the amount he thought they would have cost in Jublas. Fifty thousand Ku Rublins was the rough equivalent of twenty-five thousand Jublas. The merchant—as typical of most Kuu—was trying to cheat him.

"I think a fairer price would be one million Rublins," Flutirr said, and prepared himself for lowering his offer to eight hundred and fifty thousand. That was the price he felt to be most justified—

When the bartering was over, Flutirr wore a good pair of sturdy boots on his feet and carried six hundred thousand Ku Rublins in the form of thousands of paper bills and hundreds of heavy coins. He chafed at the poor bargain he had struck—but still, six hundred thousand Rublins was a great deal of cash. Even buying a new horse and a Dewlight's worth of supplies would use up no more than a few hundred Rublins. It would take some very expensive jewels to consume the rest. Until then, the heavy weight of the Rublins comforted him. It was true that money alone could never be a true symbol of being a Noble—it was possible for even a Tolerable to rack up a decent number of Jublas, if one became a shrewd enough merchant or a highly valued servant. Still, money was the next best thing when he no longer had boots, cape, or sword.

He found an inn and was instantly hired to play his flute for the other guests until late at night. All the market tables were, of course, closed by that time— he would have to wait until the morning to spend any of his newly obtained cash. That was just fine, Flutirr thought as he sat to begin his meal. All he wanted to do this moment was *eat*. Then perhaps he could find someone here who could guide him to a honest merchant of jewelry.

He found someone quickly—a man who may have been Human for his towering height, but whose features were vaguely Nelvin. They met after breakfast the next morning, as arranged—but before they could leave, the Human/Nelvin said: "Wait. I have invited two of my friends to join us, so we can drink at a good tavern near the merchant you want." Flutirr waited patiently with him for the man's companions to appear. When they arrived, the new pair of strangers astonished him: one was a Ku from a distant territory who—according to the Human—was buying Ku delicacies to take home. The race of the other could not be determined from his features—perhaps he came from a mixed background. Neither of the two spoke any Elvinese or Nelvinese, so all communication had to be channeled through the Human/Nelvin. How did such an odd trio develop?

The foursome left the inn together. They walked in silence for a moment, until the Human/Nelvin turned to Flutirr and said: "I am curious, Sinie-Tilll—you wear clothes that are little more than rags, yet you claim you have so many Rublins you must invest some of it in jewels. If you truly had the money, wouldn't you begin by buying things you *need*?"

Flutirr frowned—was he being accused of lying? "I do have the money—I am simply waiting until after I pay for the jewels to buy a horse and supplies."

"A horse? How can a money bag that small hold enough Rublins to buy a horse?"

"I have put my money elsewhere. My clothes may be poor, but they hide well."

"Indeed," was all the Human would say. The four turned into a long alley—a shortcut, Flutirr assumed. Then the Human stopped and turned so abruptly Flutirr almost stepped straight into his arms. "Sinie-Tilll—would you say that you have hid the money so well no thief could find it?" A strange look was in the Human's eyes. Flutirr became suddenly terrified, and took a step back. He stumbled, and a firm body behind him broke his fall—it was one of the two mysterious companions. He would have to apologize for his clumsiness—he began to turn—

Auuuoooghh! Pain, searing pain. Air—where was his air? He couldn't breathe. He groped under his chin—there was something choking him, what was it? It was taut and firm on his neck. Rope? It wasn't the right texture—and anyway, it was hurting him—

"I believe we can begin—here." The Human reached for Flutirr's belt. Flutirr froze in disbelief: he was being robbed! Then he came to his senses, and reached out to push away the groping, thieving hand— but too late, for another hand from behind him was suddenly squeezing his wrist so hard Flutirr could feel the bruises form, and the rope at his throat was pulled so tight the world became a red haze. His money bag was taken as he watched—all his Jublas, all his remaining Kuts and Kits, and thousands of Rublins.

. . . "This would be far easier if you would simply tell us where you hid the rest of your money, Sinie-

Tilll," the Human said. But, of course, Flutirr could do no such thing. He went into an insane frenzy of kicking and biting any limb that came into range—he had to get away, he had to preserve the rest of his money so he could get home—

A sharp command was uttered over his head, and Flutirr was shoved onto the ground. He struggled to stand again, but a strong fist smacked him in the back, and then his neck was held in a powerful grip. He was no longer being choked, but now he was feeling suffocated by the ground that was pressed against his face. There were sharp pebbles that dug into his skin, and he had to struggle to keep his mouth free of the dirt. Down at his waist, he could feel his flute jabbing into his body underneath him. Then the piercing scream nearly burst his sensitive Nelvin eardrums. *"Where is your money?"* Flutirr persisted; he would not tell—

There was a sudden burning pain across his back, as though he had been lashed with a horsewhip. For an insane moment, he thought: *That's* what they had around my neck. Then there was more pain, enough to drag a scream through his mouth: *"In my boots."* In less than a moment, he could feel his legs being lifted and his boots being heartlessly dragged off him. But he still couldn't get up—one of the pair from behind him had plopped down on his back, irritating his new wounds, and was still pressing his face into the dirt. Flutirr kept struggling, trying to throw him off, but he was already growing weak. Hunger no longer nagged at his stomach after his evening and morning meals, but his self-imposed starvation had weakened him.

"There is more money, Sinie-Tilll. Where is it?" Flutirr would not answer, so the weight on his back was gone, and there was more pain, burning him, throbbing in his back, until he told them: in his pants. They flipped him over. If Flutirr had been stronger and more cunning, he might have been able to use that moment to attack his attackers and escape—but he was neither of those things. They loosened his belt, got what they wanted, then turned him onto his stomach again. Once again, the invisible hand cruelly crushed his neck. There was more whipping, and the Human knelt on the ground to whisper intimately into Flutirr's ear: *C'mon, just tell us where it is, tell us and it'll all be over, yes, it'll be over, the pain will stop—*

THERE IS NO MORE MONEY, Flutirr screamed at him. YOU HAVE TAKEN EVERYTHING, he screamed—but the Human did not seem to hear. So, instead, Flutirr screamed for help, for anyone who could hear to come and stop this torture. He screamed wordlessly, and he screamed in every language he knew. He was too full of terror to wonder why no one tried to stop his screaming—he only wanted the pain to stop, stop, stop, *stop*.

There was no more weight on his neck—he could move away now, and roll away from the whip. Flutirr twitched the right muscles, but it didn't work. He tried again—but he was too weak to move anymore. The whip kept on coming, and he could not move away. He screamed again for someone to come help him—there had to be someone. He screamed again that he had no more money—they had to believe him.

No one came. No one believed him. Then, at last, the pain was over, and the trio of thieves was gone. Flutirr could move now, and return to the inn. He could clean himself, then pick up his supply bag and go home. Flutirr was free.

Trembling, he lay there for a long time.

Chapter 18

FLUTIRR was home. He was actually home.

Walking in tiny, timid steps, Flutirr crossed the bridge and approached the settlement. This was the place he had struggled to return to for so long, but now that he was here, he was afraid.

It was dusk, but there was not yet a fire. Everyone must be working. Where had Don's hut been? Disoriented, Flutirr checked every hut he came across. It was a simple task; none was locked against intruders, and all were empty. After peering into over a dozen shanties, he found one with a door that resisted his efforts to open it. Was this the one? He knocked. There was rustling, then the scraping of wood against wood, and the door opened.

"Kidder-stah. Do you need help?" A Nelvin woman stood in the doorway.

"Yes, I—is Don here? The Don who is—ill?"

"Yes. So you know of him. Where did you hear?"

Flutirr released a gasp of relief. Don was still here,

he had not been too late. "I am his friend. I have medicine to help him. He is your brother?"

"Yes—but there is no medicine that can help him."

"I do have the medicine, here in this water bottle. I don't know if it'll work, but you must let me try. I set off two Thunderballs ago to find it. I don't know if you've heard of me. I am Flutirr."

"Don told me of a Nelvin named Flutirr—but the Flutirr he told me of was a haughty High Noble who pretended to be his friend, and promised to return with medicine within a Thunderball. You, from your open face and your impassioned voice, seem more classless than Noble."

Had he changed as much as that?

"But I *am* Flutirr. I have heard Don playing his flute at the bridge just before dawn, and I am the Noble who fell into the river and was brought to your fire to warm up again—"

The woman's voice now became stiff and cold. "If you are indeed who you claim to be, then you are also the Nelvin who once threatened Don's life, as though it was worth no more than the most infertile gakkha earth."

"I am here to help him, with the medicine—just let me in, and I can begin."

The coldness did not dissipate. "Flutirr, there is a tale told by the storyteller of our town. In the tale, which he says is true, and happened many years ago, there is a little girl who becomes as ill as Don is now. Her sister cared for her, the way I am caring for

Don, until one day, the Mid Tolerable who had given the little girl a job came to the town. He claimed to have a medicine that would help the little girl, so the sister let him in the hut. He came every night for a long time to give the medicine to the child, and gained the trust of the older sister. Then, at last, he raped her—and the medicine was later found to be useless.

"How do I know I can trust you, a High Noble Don himself had said is haughty and scorns us? How do I know you did not simply go home for two Thunderballs, then created some likely-looking potion and some ragged clothes before returning? Am I to believe you went on a journey for so long to save the life of one classless Nelvin?"

"But it is not just for Don. There is more—there are enough herbs to make medicine for other Nelvins—"

"Which Nelvins? The ones of class, perhaps?"

"Classless ones too! Why, even—the boy at the Medicine-Testing Center! Kipper's son! He doesn't have to stay there anymore, he can come home and take the medicine—" Flutirr became animated now. He could see in his mind's eye the tiny wasted figure slowly coming to life again, the small brown hand of the boy reaching out to grasp his father's thick, calloused finger. Then he would be better again, and he would grow up to have children of his own—all because of a few scraps of herbs Flutirr had carried a Thunderball across the land of Trillilani. Flutirr may have appreciated Keej's gift of teaching when he received it, and he may have even thought briefly of Kipper's son receiving the cure, but only now did the idea take on solid reality for him. Soon, there would be hundreds of miracles just like this one!

The woman's expression was shifting—perhaps she was beginning to believe him at last, to agree that, yes, they should go and fetch that boy from the Medicine-Testing Center and—

"The boy is dead."

Flutirr's hand froze, mid-gesture. Dead—it was impossible, dead, impossible, no, just a little boy, no, no—and Flutirr found himself making strangling noises, so he tried to make himself stop—

The woman's angry face turned to astonishment. Then she spoke with a softer, incredulous voice.

"Flutirr, there is an expression among us, though I don't know if you Nelvins of class use it yourselves. It goes: 'I will do this, or I will do that, as soon as Nobles weep. This thing will happen, or that thing will happen, when Nobles weep.' We only use it for things we know will never happen. Have you heard of it, Flutirr?"

A little boy was dead, and she was asking about tears.

"Yes, but what of it?"

"So it is true, Flutirr, that High Nobles do not cry? Even, as we have heard, literally not to save your own lives?"

"Yes, but what does that have to do with—"

The Nelvin woman brushed her fingertips against his face. "It is not raining, is it? These are tears."

"No, those aren't—I don't—" But Flutirr could not lie because now he realized that the Nelvin was right; he was crying. Confronted with the truth, his body could not resist anymore—his crying turned into weeping.

"This is not a trick a Noblish Noble would try, so I will assume it is not a trick. You may enter, and do your best with Don. I fight well, though. If it is a trick, I'd recommend that you not enter."

Flutirr's tears kept streaming because the little boy he had never gotten to know was dead, and Don whom he did know was still in danger. But it was more because he had not cried in eighteen years, since that day so long ago when he had gotten his first gray mark at school. He had eighteen years of tears left to cry. "Thank you," he squeaked with his quivering breath. He collected the things he had put on the ground earlier, and went to kneel by Don. He prepared the first dose of medicine. Even in the dim light of the hut, he could see that Don had a ghastly yellowish color, and his eyes flickered restlessly over everything, aware of nothing. The scent of sweat, vomit, and other unidentifiable smells filled the shanty. "What is your name, Nelvin?"

"Pynnilllay."

Flutirr looked up and blinked at this Noblish name. There was no law restricting the choice of Nelvin names, but social disapproval could be as stern as any legal action. That was usually enough to discourage anyone from blending the wrong combination of sounds in a name. How could this classless Nelvin—

But of course. She had no legal existence; there was no one to keep an official record of her true name. When she went searching for jobs, she could simply use a false name—and no one would know.

"Pynnilllay," he said in confirmation, then concentrated on pouring the proper amount of the pre-steeped herbs. They were horrendously foul-smelling. He did not envy Don. "I will need a fire later to steep more herbs—there're only, I think, four or five doses in this bottle, which will last two days at the most." He clumsily tried to make the limp body before him drink some of his potion until an exasperated Pynnilllay said:

"Oh, for Nobleness's sake, let me hold him up." She shoved him aside, and sat on the floor to pull Don's head into her lap. "Now try it. Haven't you cared for the ill before?"

"No, I haven't." Flutirr had more success this time, but Don kept having minor spasms that took his mouth out of the way just as Flutirr thought he had his cup in place. Some of the medicine spilled on his clothing. "Is he always like this?"

"Sometimes it gets worse. It's part of Sporadasm, you know."

"I didn't. I mean, not that it would be this bad. He's finished with this dose."

"Then let's leave him to rest." Pynnilllay gently lowered Don's head to the ground. There was no pillow for Don to rest his head on.

"Are you not going to replace his blankets, and clean these?"

"Replace them with what? Now that Grandmother's died, he even has her blankets in there—and he'll still freeze if I take any of them away. All I can do is wash everything else that comes in contact with him, so he won't spread the Sporadasm. Which reminds me, you'd better wash that bowl, and your own hands. The river's cold, but you've got to get these things clean."

"I—I'll do that." Their grandmother dead—that must have been the elderly Nelvin woman who had been in the hut hidden under that second pile of rags two Thunderballs before. Two deaths while he had been gone; two deaths while he had been trying to save the life of one. Flutirr gathered the things he would need and went to the river, carefully marking the way.

The days passed. Flutirr and Pynnilllay tended to Don together. They gave him medicine, they fed him, they bathed him. Or, rather, Flutirr bathed him, for he felt discomfited at the thought of a female, even a sister, bathing Don's sickly sweaty body morning and night. When a neighbor gave them a ream of cloth, they sewed a new set of clothes for Don—Flutirr learned, for the first time, how to sew—and they changed him together. Then they burned the old clothes to keep the Sporadasm from spreading. It was well over a Dewlight before the fever broke.

That, Pynnilllay said, meant nothing. Part of the nature of Sporadasm was its sporadicity—it seemed to come and go. Sometimes there were spasms, sometimes not. Sometimes the patient had fever, sometimes the fever went away. Sometimes delirium and hallucinations were present, and sometimes they weren't. If Don was lucid enough to carry on a coherent conversation when he woke, then he was likely to have been cured. If not—

The anxious hours crept by. Flutirr and Pynnilllay spent, if possible, even more time in the hut than previously. They only left if necessary, to fetch food, to steep the herbs, to bathe. Don continued to sleep.

"It's getting time for his medicine," Flutirr said. Medicine was as important as sleep to Don's health, so they woke him.

"Pynnilllay," Don said softly upon wakening and seeing his sister's face.

"Oh, Don—you're lucid. We weren't sure you would be."

"We? Is Dad here? How long has it been?"

Pynnilllay nodded her head in the Trillilani gesture of negation. "Dad is probably off at work. He was lucky—he found a job for the whole season delivering messages on the nut plantation."

"He couldn't get a job planting?"

"It's the Season of Rains. Haven't you noticed the damp? And I woke you for your medicine—we think it's working."

"Medicine? Don't tell me that—Flutirr, I didn't see you." Flutirr was now by his side, with a cup filled with ill-smelling herbs.

"I've been here about a Dewlight."

"A Dewlight? Giving me that medicine?"

"And helping me care for you," Pynnilllay said. "I couldn't have gotten along without him."

"Then you really did go to the Hijj. But how did you get them to give you the medicine? Or did you trade for it?"

Flutirr cast about for some lie to tell him—wouldn't it only put a burden on Don to know of what Flutirr had done for him? Yet Don was his bonded one, even if the ceremony had been improper by Hijjian ways. Don had the right to know it.

"Among the Hijj, they only give gifts to strangers when they have some herb to give in exchange, or when they possess a bond with someone that is strong enough to demand honor from them. That includes friendship bonds. I told them that you were my friend. They gave me the medicine in honor of that bond."

"You just told them and they believed you?"

Flutirr wavered again—yet Don still had the right to know. "Friendship bonds are proven among the Hijj by bonding wounds. I made one for us."

"A bonding wound? What do you mean? Let me see it." Don was even more stubbornly persistent than Flutirr could be; Flutirr finally relented, and rolled up his sleeve. "Nobleness," Don said softly. Even after a Thunderball of healing, it was clear that the wound had not been light. Pynnilllay stepped closer to see.

"You mean you didn't get this scar with the ones on your back?"

Flutirr started. When could she have seen—

But of course. The river afforded no privacy. Anyone who bathed there could be seen by anyone who happened to look.

For an instant, Flutirr wanted desperately to share what had happened to him; he wanted to share every instant of his fear so he could, at last, shed it. But no, that was not what Don needed to hear so soon after he had recovered. He had told him of the bonding wound; that was more than enough for one weak, ill Nelvin to handle.

"Don needs his medicine," he said with sudden intensity.

Don willingly drank his herbs, then said: "Someday, I will make myself worthy of a bonding wound as deep as that."

Flutirr was speechless. "You are already worthy of it! You have taught me your music, and until I met Pynnilllay, you were my only friend."

"But surely you were friends with other Nobles?"

Flutirr's restless hands grabbed for a clump of grass to be torn apart and scattered into the breezes—but of course there was only dirt in the hut. "I—at school, I'm the only one in my class to have two gray marks. I'm also the only one in my family—I mean both the Layni-Tilll line and my mother's side, the Sinie-Wistilll line—to do that badly in school. Someone who I thought was a friend stopped speaking to me after I got the second mark." He didn't know himself why he had said all that, and of course he had to explain what a gray mark was and why it was so serious, because Don and Pynnilllay had never attended school and knew nothing of such things. Then he told Don about the day the other Nelvins had tricked him into playing the very piece that had earned him the second gray mark, just so they could be entertained by his humiliation.

"So you're here because you have no friends anywhere else?"

Flutirr looked at Don with startled discovery. "I'm here because I want to be. But maybe that *is* why I first started to come to the river."

"So you're like me."

"Like you how?"

At first Don would not answer. Then he blurted: "Even my siblings hate me."

Pynnilllay responded, "Don! You know that's not true."

"Okay, you're right, Pynnilllay—*you* love me, and the rest don't actually *hate* me—but I know that Mikul and Pinyuti, if none of the others, certainly resent me. You see, Flutirr—I can't ever do any more than get food for myself. My siblings all have to get me clothes and other things that they might otherwise be able to keep for themselves. I can't bring in extras like they can—Pinyuti got a batch of pastry sweets for us once, along with her usual pay of cloth and food, because the Low Tolerable liked her work so much. Nelvins only seem to give extras to beggars who can sing a little, and who aren't crippled like me."

"But wouldn't that—I don't understand—"

Don twisted a corner of his mouth into a crude smile, made all the cruder by the disfigurement of his lips. "You're trying to find a polite way to say that my being crippled with both a short leg and a lisp should make Nelvins pity me, and so give me more. But that doesn't alway work. Most Nelvins look at me and don't even want to see me. Perhaps being crippled makes me more real to them. They cannot so easily say to themselves that when they 'accidentally' drop their bread or nuts on the ground that the food is going nowhere for I, a classless Nelvin, do not exist. But I didn't mean to make you feel ashamed— you don't need to look like that. Perhaps we should change the subject?"

Flutirr would have responded, but Pynnilllay spoke first. "Don, Pinyuti and Mikul do *not* resent you!"

"The Nobleness they don't—they've told me themselves."

"Don, that can't be true! If they did, they must have been angry at the time. You must talk to them— I'm sure they'll—"

Don exploded. "The highest Nobleness *curse* it, Pynnilllay—don't you see? They've said it more than once. And Mikul once said that when he was younger, he used to wish I would drown in the river so everyone in the family would get more cloth to use and more food to eat. You don't know anything!"

"Oh, Don—I didn't know—"

Don attacked a corner of one of his blankets and

twisted it in his hands. "Nobleness, Pynnilllay. I'm sorry. I didn't mean for it to come out like that. I was just trying to tell Flutirr that he and I had something in common."

Something in common. Flutirr found himself tracing the path he knew his bonding scar traveled under his sleeve. Friends were supposed to have things in common. Even if they were painful things, like having the very people who ought to care about you the most resenting you instead.

"My parents don't resent me the way Mikul and Pinyuti resent you, Don—but I know they won't be happy to see me when I go home," Flutirr said. Then he heard his last few words and thought, Oh Nobleness. That would have to be soon, wouldn't it? Don was recovered now—there was little more for Flutirr to do—

"Flutirr! They'll be crazy with anxiety about you. All parents love their children."

"I'm too old to have the appeal of a child, Don. And I have two gray marks. They almost Disowned me for that, you know. Maybe Father would be happy to have me keep up the Tilll line, and Mother would rather have her Secondary name passed on than nothing at all. But that's really it."

"And I've always thought you had everything," Don said quietly.

"I used to envy *you,* because you could play music the way you liked, not the way your parents and teachers said you should. I think no one has everything."

"Seems like it," Don said.

There was a moment of heavy silence, then, in a burst of long-pent-up frustration, Flutirr said: "If only we didn't have these cursed classes, and there weren't any Nobles or classless ones. Then my parents wouldn't be so ashamed of me, and you could—you could even be a Professional Musician! You wouldn't have to be a beggar anymore."

"Things have always been like that, Flutirr. It doesn't do anything to think about the other ways things could be."

Flutirr's first instinct was to agree. He had been trained by years of being told that the class system was irrevocable, and that was the way things ought to be. Then something in him rebelled.

"No! I can change things! I will be on the Council in about—oh, I've forgotten. I've turned twenty-four years old already. That means it's just a little under three Thunderballs until I'm on the Low Council, and a few more years until I can introduce bills on the High Council. If I make the right bills—"

"But how would you get anyone to listen to you if you have those two gray marks? And how will you get anyone to believe that they should treat classless ones like Nelvins of class when we are not even supposed to exist?"

Flutirr was silent with a sudden flooding of shame. He had spent two Thunderballs and a Dewlight struggling to shed the last of his Noblish ways—yet he had just fallen prey to the blind belief that it would be easy for him to cause change simply because he was a High Noble. Don was right. It was not enough to write bills and introduce them. He had to convince literally thousands of Nelvins of class that all of them had to treat one another as Nelvins—not pairs of colors, or pairs of boots and fancy swords and capes. The beliefs of Nelvin society had taken millennia to develop. It would take so long to reverse such ancient patterns that Flutirr would not even live to see the end of what he started.

Yet he had to try. He had to try for all the Nelvins in the district of Trilene who lived under oppression—whether the oppression of Noblish ways or the oppression of being classless. And more than that—he had to try for Don. He had to try for his bonded friend.

"I have the medicine. I can share it with the Medicine-Testing Center—I want to share it with them anyway. The Council members would have to listen to me then, as the Nelvin who saved thousands of lives from the disease of Sporadasm. I—I can at least begin to make change."

"So you'll have to go home tomorrow, won't you?"

Tomorrow? Why tomorrow? They had just become friends. They had just gotten to know each other. Certainly Flutirr had to leave soon—but not so fast. Not tomorrow.

But Flutirr knew with a sudden, aching lurch that Don was right. For each day Flutirr lingered, there would be another Nelvin somewhere in Trilene, or elsewhere in the Centre of Nelvins, who died because no one knew of a medicine for Sporadasm. The sooner Flutirr returned home, the more Nelvins he could save. Flutirr had a duty to perform.

Before Flutirr could share his newfound commitment, however, Don said: "Flutirr—I'm tired." And, indeed, he now seemed frighteningly pale. He was recovering, but his health was not fully restored.

"Nobleness, I'm sorry. I've worn you out—I shouldn't have talked so much. You'd better sleep now, then we can say good-bye to each other in the morning."

Wearily, Don nodded. He promptly snuggled deeper into his blankets and fell asleep. Flutirr was struck by how much like a small, sleeping boy Don's slight figure and fragile features seemed. Impulsively, he pressed a hand against Don's face—but, of course, the fever was still gone.

"Flutirr." Pynnilllay's voice was softer than it needed to be. He turned. "Flutirr, I will be going to the nut plantation early in the morning to try to find a job. We have to say good-bye before going to sleep."

Flutirr stopped himself just in time from making a sharp-tongued comment on how quickly Pynnilllay planned to leave Don. Classless ones could never afford to be unemployed for even a single day. It was already bad enough that Don and Pynnilllay's family had had to suffer without the food that either of the pair could have earned during the two Thunderballs of Don's illness. Instead, Flutirr said good-bye, and he even endured the brief touch of her hand on his cheek.

No, he had not endured it—he had enjoyed the soft, ephemeral, feminine touch.

"Good night," Pynnilllay said. It was evening now, and time for bed.

Flutirr abruptly realized that just the following night he would be at home in his own mansion, sleeping in an actual bed—not on the bare ground. And he would be able to look up at the ceiling again, and see the portraits of all his ancestors gazing grimly down upon him, as though checking his every motion for the least trace of unNoblishness.

It had been a long, emotionally draining day, and Flutirr was tired. He lay on the ground to sleep beside his two classless friends.

He woke to see Don leaning over him. All of a sudden, it was time to go home—

Flutirr pulled himself from the ground. *I don't want to go,* he almost said. *I don't want to leave home.*

The pair of Nelvins stood, awkwardly facing each other. How in the land of Trillilani could they say good-bye?

Don looked so small, Flutirr thought. And should he be standing so soon after being ill? Then he saw a tiny, scrawny hank of hair mournfully peering over a sea of hair above Don's forehead.

"Your hair's sticking out," he said lamely. He moistened his fingers, and valiantly struggled to tame the cowlick.

"Flutirr, it's always sticking up. You just haven't seen it before."

Were they going to say their farewells by talking about Don's hair?

"I—I will visit—I'll be bringing food and—" Flutirr stumbled over the words, and couldn't say anything more. Of *course* he would visit, and of *course* he would bring food. What he needed were words that somehow encompassed the full turmoil of emotions he felt in him—

Don suddenly pulled Flutirr into a hard hug. It was an alien, enveloping sensation Flutirr had not known for eighteen years—and it said everything he wanted to say. He hugged Don back, and they stood that way for a long time—

The hug broke.

"I—" Flutirr started to say, but stopped. His hug had said everything. He studied Don's face for the last time—

No, no—not for the last time. He was going to visit.

But, of course, it could never be the same again. Once Flutirr entered the city, he could no longer be like the classless ones—the danger would be too great. He could never hug anyone, or be anyone's friend the way he was Don's friend. He could come back to visit, but only as a Noblish Noble coming to see an inferior Nel—

Don was crying.

Crying? For Flutirr?

Don gave him a wet, tremulous smile. "Hey, Flutirr—you're crying like a classless one."

Mutely, Flutirr raised a hand to his face. Yes, he was. For the moment, at least, he was classless. He was classless and free.

ANDREA SHETTLE, winner of the 1989 Avon Flare Young Adult Novel Competition, was born in Madison, Wisconsin, and was raised in Wellesley, Massachusetts. She is a student at Gallaudet University in Washington, D.C., the only liberal arts university in the world for deaf students.

Writing is a major interest for Ms. Shettle, who won many prizes for her short stories while in high school. *Flute Song Magic* is her first novel. Other interests include activism for issues important to her, mostly related to deaf rights, and working with children. She is also an avid reader, with a particular interest in science fiction and fantasy.